Clearwater's Savior

Tiffany Casper

Mountain Of Clearwater

Wrath MC

Book 1

Copyright © Tiffany Casper 2020

All rights reserved. No part of this publication may be reproduced, distributed, or transmitted in any form or by any means, including photocopying, recording, or other electronic or mechanical methods, without the prior written permission of the publisher, except in the case of brief quotations embodied in critical reviews and certain other noncommercial uses permitted by copyright law.

Dedication

For the people who are struggling with this epic time in all of our life's that we seem to be on a spin cycle with. I hope this book allows you a brief escape from your day-to-day life.

As for my family thank you so much for allowing me to work with only minimal interruptions that come with kids that are both under the age of ten.

Editor = Rebecca Vazquez

Cover Design = Tiffany Casper

As always, thank you to Tammy Carney my PA. I wouldn't be where I am without you!

Shutterstock Photographer = German Gonzalez Stock

Thank you for cherry sour gummies world, they are awesome. I wanted to give a special thanks to my readers. Without y'all, none of this would even be possible, and thank you for leaving reviews. If I don't take in what y'all say, then these books no doubt would be crappy. So, thank you for taking time out of your day to write a review and for allowing your thoughts to be heard.

Wrath MC

Original

Clearwater Chapter

Cotton – President

York – Vice President

Garret – Enforcer

Cooper – Sgt. At Arms

Xavier – Secretary

Dale – Treasurer

Walker – Road Captain

Knox – Icer

Playlist

Midnight Rider – Allman Brothers

Collide – Howie Day

Bullet In A Bonfire – Brantley Gilbert

Just Hold On – Savannah Dexter Ft. Adam Calhoun

Night Moves – Bob Segar

Without You – Upchurch Ft. Rizzi Myers

TABLE OF CONTENTS

PREQUEL

PROLOGUE

CHAPTER 1

CHAPTER 2

CHAPTER 3

CHAPTER 4

CHAPTER 5

CHAPTER 6

CHAPTER 7

CHAPTER 8

CHAPTER 9

CHAPTER 10

CHAPTER 11

CHAPTER 12

CHAPTER 13

EPILOGUE

THANK YOU

OTHER WORKS

CONNECT WITH ME

Prequel

Wrath MC

The most notorious, dangerous, one-percenter motorcycle club isn't the one everyone knows about. It isn't the one everyone sees at rallies, charity events, or even at bars. Some say Wrath MC is just a myth. A club that was savage, a club that passed around women then sold them to the highest bidder. Others say the MC is full of nine to fivers and weekend warriors. They also say, no one wanted to cross them. Well, some of those myths just may be true. While there are rumors about the club and those are galore, the rumor of where the mother charter could possibly be located is the largest one of all.

The people in a little old county in North Carolina know better. The three hundred square miles in Clearwater held a secret. A very well-known secret or two. Little did they know, Wrath MC holds many more secrets, a lot of those are made of stories your momma warned you about.

Some people have even been rumored to have gone missing in the area, never to be heard from again.

While others have either passed through and are but a fading memory, some have come and gone and left their mark. While others have come and made their mark on not only the MC but on the community as well.

This story is about one of the members of Wrath MC—the President, to be exact.

Hold on for one wild alpha badass man and a romance that will last till the end of time.

Prologue

'Life gives you lemons.

Make Lemonade.'

Novalie

What had passed through their minds when they were children? Bronte, Sparks, Meyer, Ashley? Was it dreams of what they would become, world-famous authors? Did they have such a great childhood full of fairy tales and the willingness to learn and defy the laws of what people could be or do? What about Shakespeare, who revolutionized the Sixteenth and the Seventeenth centuries with his works, works that still to this day are part of the curriculum in school because they made history. What about the fact that every year a play is made and performed to one of his works?

Or did Meyer envision that the plan and thought process of her writing would become a household name in *Twilight* and that it would go on to make millions among millions? And all of that in a world where fantasies such as hers were only ever whispered about. People didn't foresee a book like hers hitting the big screen, and yet when it did, it changed the whole playing field.

I bet Sparks didn't intend for his romance novels to be on the shelves of almost every major retailer, not only in the country but the world.

And as I sat there in English class, I wondered if maybe authors like King are brilliant rather than crazy as so many have called him. He has reached a magnitude that some other individuals and not even authors have reached or possibly may never achieve.

What would it take to be that great? Was it in their literary works? Or was it possible they had become so content and so happy in their lives that the words just flowed to them?

The bell ending fourth period snapped me out of the reverie of a seventeen-year-old mind.

It was time to go home. Home to an empty house with empty cabinets. I didn't even feel like I was truly at home in that house. It was just four walls. I wondered what a house I was able to call home would feel like.

Shouldn't a home be where you felt the safest? Where you feel like you could do and be anything?

Luckily, today was Thursday, and seeing as we have a three-day weekend, school was over.

Since there was usually a lot of activity at the clubhouse, especially since tomorrow was my mother and stepfather's second anniversary according to them.

They say they celebrated the day they met for the first time and the day that they were married.

It was a prelude to tomorrow for my mom and stepdad's "anniversary". Oh well. Hopefully, they have a good time. They should since they celebrated it twice a year after all.

Even so, since they don't celebrate the actual event that happens on that date every year.

Luckily, I only had nine more days after that and finally, I would be graduating high school and hopefully going to college and be able to provide a better life for myself.

Where had my so-called parents been in all of this you ask? Probably on another weekly adventure of theirs. But I knew it like the back of my hand, they were at the clubhouse and planning on spending tonight and tomorrow night there in my stepdad's room. Then more than likely they would be gone again.

I still don't understand how my stepdad still held his patch with Wrath MC, except that Cotton was a forgiving man. Well, I had only ever seen the nice side of him.

But I had heard stories, a lot of stories, that told about a violent and dangerous man. A man you didn't cross, and if you did, you wouldn't get very far. You didn't become the president of an MC and one of the most feared men on the east coast just because you were nice to everyone you encountered.

"June!" I called out as soon as I saw my closest friend. I didn't really want to walk all the way to the clubhouse from school. Not on today, of all days.

Heck, I normally had to walk half a mile to school and back home again if I couldn't catch a ride with June.

When I had a shift at the diner, the cook always gave me a ride home. And when Virginia had found that out, she had started picking me up on the weekends when I had a shift.

"Hey, girl." June was, for all intents and purposes, the one person at this school who I could talk to and who would understand. I had made June promise to not call Child Protective Services a bunch of times when I had to show up at school wearing the same clothes as the day before.

I hadn't wanted to be placed in foster care, not when I'd heard too many horror stories. It wasn't that the MC didn't help, but they didn't know it had gotten as bad as it was. No, it wasn't terrible, but I knew it could be a lot worse.

Once a week, my parents made sure to stock the fridge so when they were not there, I had been able to at least eat. However, ever since the day I had turned twelve that had all changed. They had stopped putting food in the house.

If it weren't for June and being able to eat lunch at school, I hated to think where I would have been at the tender age of twelve. More than likely I would have starved.

It was a wonder they even remembered to keep the rent paid, never mind the electricity. Virginia had been my saving grace in many ways, giving me a job under the table doing small things for me and then hiring me on at her diner when I had turned sixteen.

"Can I catch a ride with you?" I knew June wouldn't mind. Heck, any time I had asked her for anything if it was in her power, June had helped me. Not to mention June gets upset with me when I don't ask for help.

"Sure. Where to?" Like always, I was extremely lucky to have June in my life.

"The clubhouse, please and thank you," I said with a smile.

"No problem. Let's get out of here." We were both graduating next week and it was going to be a great reprieve to not have to deal with the idiots who populated our high school.

Especially seeing as a lot of the boys were perverts and thought that they knew everything and that they were hot stuff.

Yeah . . . no. According to me, and maybe the entire female population, only one man stood out in my mind and no one could even hold a candle stick to that man. Was he older than me? Yes, by like a lot, but God puts us on this earth for a reason.

And Cotton's reason was to give every single woman, and some men, a living and breathing dream man in the flesh.

The man was six-foot-two, long and strong, in all the right places. Whereas I was five-foot-three on a good day.

His upper half was covered in tattoos, I knew, but I'd never seen what was beneath the shirt. He rarely had it off at the clubhouse unless it was fight night and I had always worked during those times.

His hair was almost a deep honey brown, but it looked blonde in the light, and it was half as long as my own, though he always wore it up in a man bun. And where I had blue eyes, his were a vivid honey color.

I knew from just hanging out in the shadows that more often than not the women who had been caught in his stare, usually melted into a pool of desire.

After we had gotten into June's Jeep and buckled up, I cranked up the tunes. Luckily, Clearwater was warm enough in May to have the top off. Being young and in the country, that was the life. We both felt as if we were the epitome of VSCO girls like out in California but on the east coast.

Once we'd arrived at the clubhouse ten minutes later, I climbed out and said, "Thanks, girl."

"No problem. Enjoy your weekend." June had been pulling away from me in the past couple of months, and I still had no idea what was up with that.

June's mom had been killed in a bad car accident when she was thirteen. If it hadn't been for an older neighbor, June would have been placed in foster care.

"Same." I then allowed my wonderful working nose to lead the way to the back of the clubhouse where the smells of burgers, ribs, and hotdogs permeated the air.

"Novalie," my drunk mom called out. Really, at five after three in the afternoon? That wasn't new . . . unfortunately.

"Hey, Mom," I murmured, already dreading this conversation, especially when the ending would always be the same. Whatever I had to say to her would go in one ear and out the other.

It's supposed to go the other way, that whatever the parent says to the teenager goes in one way and out the other. But not for me. I swore my brain was always on a power trip. I could usually read something one time and then turn around and recite it word for word like a year later.

"Come, give your momma a hug. It's been so long since I've seen you. Twelve looks good on you," she slurred out. Yeah, good going, Mom.

I definitely didn't have the body of a twelve-year-old girl any longer. I had curves that made a lot of the boys at school stop in the hallway and turn their heads.

Which then caused me to hate my figure, so I always wore baggy clothes to school to help ease that away whenever I could. Well, depending on the weather.

Luckily, it was hottest in the summer months and we didn't have school, so I was able to wear what I wanted. I didn't have to worry about the boys from school seeing me since they all more than likely had a life.

Sure, I had a life, but that life revolved a lot around the MC and the events they held.

"Yeah, Mom. Listen, I need you to pick me up early on Wednesday after a test, and then on Saturday, I have graduation."

My mom, Amy, took in a puff of smoke before she said anything. "What time?" she asked, then blew said smoke directly in my face, like she didn't care that as a child I had dealt with bad asthma attacks. To this day, I had to carry a rescue inhaler with me.

And the Mother of the Year award goes to Amy, I thought sarcastically.

"Wednesday, I need to be picked up at eleven. And Saturday, I need to be at school at ten in the morning for graduation."

"Okay," she slurred again while inhaling another puff of smoke that had her eyes appearing dazed and confused.

"Great, Mom," I muttered to myself. "Are you going to remember those times, or do I need to write them down for you?"

I wasn't trying to be a snob, but it was important that I at least tried to reiterate to her about the dates and times. At least it showed that one of us was trying to keep some semblance of a family, a broken one but still a family, nonetheless.

My family was broken because I had learned when I was eight that the man I had thought was my father wasn't really my father at all but the man my mother had cast a spell on, in a sense.

I would say that the reason my mother wanted nothing to do with me was because of my stepdad, French, but that was so far from the case, it wasn't even funny.

I'd heard them arguing after social services had shown up at our house after a teacher reported the fact that I'd been going to school in the same clothes for a week at a time. Also, because I had been skin and bones quite a few times.

It had also been a teacher who had sent me to the nurse's station one morning to have them take a look at my arm.

Some cat had been dumb enough to climb up a tree that it couldn't get down. So, me being as I was, loving animals, and being a twelve-year-old who thought I was invincible, climbed the tree and coaxed the cat down. All for it to claw at me like I'd thrown it in a bucket of water.

When I'd swatted at the cat, trying to make it stop, I'd lost my balance and fallen out of the tree. My arm ended up breaking my fall. Quite literally.

Still to this day, my own mother didn't know a word about that. The woman who covered that medical bill had been Virginia. It had been Virginia who they had called when they hadn't been able to reach my mom.

"I always look out for you. I am your mother after all." Who the heck was she trying to convince?

I wanted to yell at her that she'd never looked out for me. However, I knew it would fall on deaf ears. No matter what I said to my mother, it never penetrated. And when it did, my mother just didn't give a damn about me. How was that possible given that she had carried me for nine months?

Instead of dwelling on my mother, I wandered my way to the tables where all the food was laid out. I didn't want to seem like a pig, but God, all the smells were assaulting my senses like there was no tomorrow.

"Novalie," Cotton said over my shoulder. Suddenly, a melting sensation hit my entire frame. The sound of my name coming from his mouth . . . Jesus.

Yes, he was a lot older than me, but that didn't deter me in the least. Never would I act on my feelings unless he gave me some kind of inkling that he thought age was just a number too.

However, since that wasn't likely to happen, if I were ever to find a man, I wanted him to be a lot like Cotton.

Then something unthinkable happened—he handed me a slice of my favorite pie, strawberry swirled cheesecake.

"What's this for?" I didn't hold back like a lot of people did when they talked to Cotton.

Sure, I had only spoken to him a few times, but those times that I did, I knew without a shadow of a doubt that he would never hurt me. I didn't get that same vibe from some of my stepdad's so-called friends and his brothers, but I did from Cotton.

And that meant something to me. That meant a lot.

"I grabbed too damn much," he said as he looked down at me.

And the moment our eyes locked, I felt desire swimming through my veins.

"You've got room for it. You sure you don't want it?" *Okay, wow, girl, way to say he looked fat*, I chided myself.

"Darlin', I got a figure to watch." With a wink, he chuckled as he meandered away from me and the buffet-style tables.

Despite his age, he still looked good. I wasn't attracted to the boys at school. They were still just ick. They were adolescents. A lot of French's brothers were very good-looking, but none of them held a candle to Cotton.

Ever seen the movie *Aquaman*? You know the actor who plays Arthur, a hunk of a beast named Jason Momoa? No? Well, watch the first ten minutes of the movie. There's Cotton.

Though you'd have to add a little more length to his honey brown hair that was half as long as my own, and a lot more tattoos. He even had the whole neatly trimmed beard thing going on.

Sure, I wasn't even legal yet, but I was about to turn eighteen and a girl knows what looks good and what doesn't.

Talk about gorgeous with a capital G.

I stared down at the slice of cheesecake and wavered. How could one simple slice of cheesecake mean so much to me?

I shook my head to clear my mind, reminding myself to not look too much into it. Yes, it was one of the only things that I'd ever been given, but still.

I carried my plates over to a nearby tree, sat down with my back against the trunk, and dug in. I ate the slice of cheesecake first, how could I not?

As I was chewing on a rib, one of the other daughters, Creedence, better known as Cree, came over to my spot.

"Hey, girl," Cree said as she sat and ate her own plate full of food.

"Hey, Cree. How are you?" Though I was five years older, Cree was perhaps the only person in the whole MC who I was even remotely close to.

All the brothers talked to Cree, but rarely, if ever, did they talk to me. The only one who really talked to me was Cotton, even if it was just the barest conversation.

How sad was that?

"Doing okay. Struggling in math though." Cree wasn't alone with that at all.

"Oh, I'm sorry. I don't like math either. But I can try to help if you need me to." No idea how I could really help her, but I knew that any time you offered your help, at least you put yourself out there.

"Thanks, girl, but that's okay. Dad's looking into getting me a tutor. Though the first two that have come to the house have been all eyes for my dad. He even closed the door in one of their faces when they batted their eyelashes at him." It was funny when Cree scrunched her nose for emphasis.

"Dang, that's harsh," I said as we laughed.

"I mean, I know my dad is good-looking because, well, hey, look at me, but ewe."

I was still laughing at her. Sure, her dad, Garret, was good-looking, but he had nothing on Cotton.

"Well, if it isn't the princess of the MC and the throwaway." And there was one of the bad seeds of the MC. Justin was one year older than me, and in fact, he was prospecting for the MC.

But I didn't really see him getting the approval from Cotton. Hopefully not.

"Go away, Justin," Cree said.

"It's a free country," the pecker head stated.

Nobody really liked Justin. Why, just last week he'd told me that I needed to start riding the short bus. Did his parents not care that he was a jerk?

"It's only a free country for girls, not for boys," I told him.

"Nobody asked you," Justin said snidely.

Then Justin turned his full attention to Cree, "Little miss Creedence, you're looking hot today—" He didn't get to finish his sentence because I didn't like the way he'd just spoken to my friend. So, thanks to watching some kick-ass movies that showed women literally kicking ass, I brought my foot up and kicked it out, nailing Justin right in the balls.

"You bitch!" he stammered out, clutching at his balls while his face became pale.

Before Justin could retaliate, Cotton was there.

"What the fuck?" Cotton didn't look mad. I could tell that he was agitated, but the little lift in the corner of his mouth was all I really needed to know.

"Ask the bit—" Justin didn't get to finish that statement because Cotton had his hand on Justin's throat as he applied pressure, which you could see exactly how much pressure from the veins that were protruding in Cotton's hand.

"Want to rethink your damn vocabulary?" he snarled out. Now, that little lift at the corner of his mouth was all one straight line.

Justin was shaking his head in response.

Before he let Justin go, Cotton looked at me, I saw his eyes soften the smallest inch.

"Want to tell me why you kicked him in the balls?" I couldn't be sure, but I also saw a hint of something comical in his gaze. Kind of like he was holding back from laughing. Then his little smile reappeared as I gave him my answer.

"Cotton, it wasn't her—" Cotton put his hand up, wanting Cree to stop talking.

Cree, Justin, and myself weren't the only ones witnessing our altercation either.

"Novalie." There it was, his 'no argument' tone. Many men had been subdued when he used that tone.

"He . . ." I took in a breath. Why was this so hard? It wasn't like this was the first time I'd talked to Cotton, but it was the first time that his tone and his stare had been directed squarely at me. "He said Creedence . .

. and everyone knows she hates being called that, but that wasn't why I got upset. He said she was looking hot today. She's only twelve. He had no right looking at her like she was a piece of meat and a club slut," I said, biting my quivering bottom lip.

It wasn't in anyone's place who wasn't a brother or an ole' lady to attack a brother or even a prospect. That was one of the rules in Wrath MC.

But what I did notice, as everyone else had, was that he didn't bother to ask Justin if that was true, nor had he even bothered to confirm with Cree.

He always double-checked with everyone and everything when he was meting out justice based on the facts. And he always based everything on facts, never opinions.

All of that showed that he trusted my word, and for an MC president, and for Cotton, that was huge.

With his hand around Justin's throat, he carried him away and threw him at his dad.

"Teach that little bastard some god damn manners," Cotton told Easley, Justin's father.

Off in the distance, we all heard Easley laying into Justin. Did I think it would work? Probably not. Would it be great if it did? Yes.

With that, Cotton walked away, talking on his cell when it rang after he had thrown Justin at his dad.

"You okay, sweetheart?" Garret, Cree's dad, kneeled in front of her.

"Yeah, Daddy." Then Cree turned her head and said, "Thanks, Novalie."

With that, I just smiled and said, "Us girls have to stick together. Besides, we always have each other's back."

"Thanks, Novalie, it would seem you try to have everyone else's back even though most don't return the favor," Garret said to me, and yet no more was said or mentioned. Kind of like it was left hanging in the air that he knew, but no one bothered to do a thing about it.

I said my same old response, "No problem," as I saw all the worrying and confused glances directed at Cree.

But as Cree's dad glanced at me with a smile, no one else had bothered to check on me. No one seemed to ever have my back, but that was okay. I'd been on my own since I was twelve.

I looked around and saw my mom and French as they were carrying on, laughing, and not once did either of them bother to come over to check on things.

Like it would've mattered had they done that or not. I wasn't jealous or hateful. To be honest, I'd kind of gotten used to being the odd one out.

What I didn't know was that afternoon, I'd earned a nickname from one of the members in the MC. And it was from the one who was so intent on watching me, though I hadn't even noticed.

Only one other person on the grounds had seen a hint of emotion written all over that person's face. Had I noticed that the other person watching the rest of the moment played out, I would've been wary.

And I would've been on guard for something that was about to upend the rest of my life.

Chapter 1

'When your whole world gets rocked,

Rock with it.'

Cotton

"Alright, church is in session." I banged the gavel to my right where I sat at the head of the table.

It was all thanks to my grandfather, who had left me this space on the day I had turned eighteen. My grandfather, Greg O'Malley, passed away one week after my birthday. It was him who taught me all about motorcycles and the love for them, and it was also my grandfather who had taken me on my first ride when I had turned two.

Ever since then, I've had a passion for them, and in return, it has given me a life to love.

The entire space sat on a parcel of my ten acres of land. We also had a five-bay garage where we had one bay for bikes only, a bay for jacked-up trucks, a bay for standard SUVs and trucks, and two for cars. Attached to the garage was our clubhouse. It was all brick, built back in nineteen-seventy-nine.

We had done a major remodel and gutted out a lot of the inside, but the outside structure was sturdy and strong, if I was being honest, I loved that it was weathered, torn, and damaged but still standing strong. A lot like myself in that regard and many of my brothers as well.

In the clubhouse, on the main floor, we had a main room with a bar, pool tables, a dance floor, a pole, and a few dart boards. We had three couches that had seen better days and tables and chairs. There was a full kitchen with double Dutch ovens, which came in handy for all our parties and events. We had a laundry room for all the brothers. My office was on the main floor, along with our room for church and a bathroom for all the masses to use.

The second floor housed the prospects' three rooms on the left. On the right, there were three rooms for the club girls and a shared bathroom for them all.

On the third floor, we had eight rooms, one for each of the top club members, with a bathroom for each of them.

But if the club kept going the way we were, we were going to have to add another building for more rooms. We were selective as all get out and it took a lot for someone to become a member. The standard prospect run was twelve months with other clubs, but with ours, it is two years.

Hence why we'd branched out and established a sister chapter in Dogwood, Tennessee. We were also in the process of starting up in the surrounding states including South Carolina, but that would take time.

In the room where we held church, that was the room that was the most sacred in the entire building. Hell, possibly on the entire plot of land.

We had a table that one of my buddies made and carved our logo on. It was simple. It was Lucifer.

Why had I based my club around the devil? Because I wanted people to fear me and my brothers. Fear us in a way that when we walked into a room, people stood stock still. Another part of that was that I wanted people to leave us the fuck alone.

In doing so, we ran guns, we saved women who were being trafficked, and we rescued people from abusive situations when the system failed them. We called them Doves. Simple as fuck.

Oh, and we were Harley enthusiasts.

Luckily, we also had some silent investors that only the club officers knew about.

We were able to launder the gun money through the garage and the custom jobs we did.

Was it illegal? You're damn right. But did I go to sleep easy each and every single night knowing that myself and my brothers were actually living and not struggling? You're damn right.

Not to mention we always had to stay at the top of our game. Way too many clubs and assholes had been trying to take over our supply and our pipeline.

"First order of business, did the new girl get to her new location?" I asked my Vice President, York.

"Yeah, confirmed with Powers last night before he and some of the club headed this way for the weekend party." York had only been back in the States for three years. Some bad shit had happened to him and he still had no fucking clue what all had really transpired while he was in the military. Something he endured over there had caused him to lose his memory.

Fuck, the only way he even knew about me and the MC was because Cooper had shown him pictures of all of them back in the day. There was only one person who'd been omitted from the pictures, which had been hard to do, seeing as she'd been in almost every single one. The two of them had been inseparable. His story was something else.

"Right. Second-order of business, I've been noticing some cash has been going missing. Anyone know anything about that?"

"I've got a look at the books. Everything is tight," French slurred out. He was already drinking.

Since it was his and his ole' lady, Amy's, anniversary that night, we were going to be knee-deep to our asses in food, booze, and pussy.

"Alright, everyone, keep an eye out. I know good and damn well that Lucy ain't the one stealing from the register. She's loyal to a fault."

Dale's face was glowing. He'd picked a good one in her. Matter of fact, he was the only one in the club besides French who even had an ole' lady. Lucy was in a club all by herself though. No one ever gave Amy the respect garnered from being an ole' lady.

"Anything else we need to talk about before we have a fucking party?"

Fists pounded the table at the insinuations that were being made.

"Alright, church is closed," I said as I slammed the gavel back down.

Everyone exited the room, going this way and that way, getting everything ready for tonight.

I knew French and his ole' lady always celebrated their anniversary on the last Saturday in May. Only for the life of me, I couldn't remember why they celebrated their anniversary twice a year.

As the music played and food disappeared off the tables, everyone had beers in their hands and bodies were moving on the dance floor. The place was fucking packed.

We even had a few members there from another club who had been looking into becoming Wrath MC.

33

The idea of being illegal yet still making it in the world without the FBI on our asses was high and large. So, we had to keep a tight-ass ship like always. We didn't even want to be on their radar.

The President of our Dogwood chapter—and one of my closest friends—Powers had made the drive. He had brought with him five of his brothers, Cam, his VP, Heathen, his untouchable Enforcer, Linc, their tech guru, Axel, and Skinner, their silent badass.

A few other members who had gone rogue even showed up for the party. It wasn't for French and Amy, though. No, it was for the booze, the women, and the food. All precisely in that order.

As I sat there at the edge of the bar nursing my beer, I watched the party as it was going on in full force, but there was only one person at the clubhouse who wasn't having a good time.

I thought back to yesterday. Before I could get over there to make sure she was okay, because no one bothered to even check on her, Novalie had left. A phone call that lasted two fucking damn hours had kept me from that.

In all actuality though, tonight she looked plain miserable. Tonight's expression was the worst that I'd ever seen on her pretty face.

I didn't know how old she was, and I wasn't even going to go there, but something deep in my gut niggled at me every single time I thought about her.

Something about her stirred a sensation deep inside of me that I'd never felt before, and it was all because of Novalie, the daughter of French and his ole' lady, Amy.

Everyone knew that French wasn't her real father, but he was the only father she'd ever known. She didn't call him 'dad' or 'father', but French, and that had seemed off to him.

She'd been coming to the clubhouse for these events and then some. She seemed like she really enjoyed life and living within the MC family. But on nights like tonight, I wasn't so sure.

I had noticed when she walked in the door that she had a frown on her face, and that was the last I'd seen of her.

Then, I saw when she went out back to the courtyard earlier.

Not to mention I highly doubted if some or if any of my brothers even knew her name, but that was ridiculous—she was family after all.

It wasn't the fact that she was drop-dead gorgeous or anything that had caused me to amble out to the back of the clubhouse. Nor was it because someone in the clubhouse had needed me.

No, it was the simple fact that she was shy, sassy at times, and had a weird cuteness to her that drew me in.

I took in the back of the courtyard, in search of her because I hadn't seen her in the main room while the cheers and well-wishes had been going on.

There, to my left, she was swaying in the hammock—his hammock—reading a book.

In. My. Hammock. A hammock that no one dared to get in. The clubhouse had five areas that no one else was allowed in without explicit invitation.

The first was my bedroom. No other female had been in there—I always went to their rooms. The second place was my office. The third area that was all mine was in my hammock. The fourth area was a shelf in the kitchen. Most of the brothers tried to get into it, but I kept that shit locked down. I fucking counted each and every one of those Little Debbie cakes. The fifth was my house. That was fucking mine.

Strange, but the same sensations that assaulted me whenever someone had even contemplated facing my fury by getting near my hammock were completely gone. For her, for some unknown and strange reason, I didn't mind.

Not one single bit.

How she managed to keep track of where she was on a page of that book she was reading all the while gently swaying had been beyond him. Hell, he still had to focus on keeping his place while standing still, or even sitting for that matter, whenever he had been reading something.

"Want to tell me why you're out here and not in there?" I thumbed behind me toward the main room.

A shrug was all I got in reply.

Not giving up that easy, I asked, "They upset you or something?"

Not a shrug to that statement, but silence. Okay.

"Seems to me, if it were my parents' anniversary, I'd be in there celebrating with them."

That time, I received more than a shrug . . . I got a "hmm".

"Must be nice that your parents are still alive, not like others. Not like mine."

Again, no reaction, but I did notice the way her eyes narrowed, and her mouth tightened just a pinch more.

As I stood there thinking what could really get a reaction from this silent one, a thought occurred to him.

"Did they not get you your dream car? Did they not buy you everything you ever wanted? Did they not love you enough?"

Either she was tired of me saying things, or she just got fed up with me being there, she closed her book and sat it on her chest that was rising with her every breath.

No, I was wrong. Dead wrong. Novalie was getting pissed. I had seen her angry before, but never pissed. And it was a sight to behold.

I then turned rock hard, which I had to tamper down immediately. She was a fucking baby.

"No" was all she murmured while she stared up at the night sky.

"No? No to which part?" It took all that I had to hold back the smile that was wanting to burst forth.

"Are we really doing this, Pres?" She lifted to a sitting position as she was viewing me with a cynical eye. Her eyes had the fires of hell burning in them.

Normally, I didn't blink an eye when those associated with the club called me Pres. But that word coming from her mouth, I didn't like it, not one bit.

"Yeah, I guess we are." I was going to get to the bottom of this.

I wanted to know why she was mostly always silent, why she didn't party with her parents when they were celebrating, and why, for some unholy reason, she always had her nose stuck in some book or another.

"Well, Mr. Nosy Pants, for your information, I stopped celebrating my parents' anniversary on today's date when I was born." And she wasn't done either.

"And also for your information, the last things my parents bought for me were groceries when I was twelve." She had no idea how badly I wanted to wipe away the tears that were now surfacing in the corners of her eyes, until she looked away from me.

For the first time in my life, I wanted to kiss away every single tear that trailed down her cheeks. Now, how sick was that? I was an old son of a bitch and she was what, probably fifteen?

Still, I rocked back on my heels, unsure of what to say or even think for that matter, after those statements left her mouth.

What did she mean they haven't bought her anything since she was twelve? She was in clothes that fit her, and she didn't look like she'd been starving. And what had that born comment meant?

"Then tell me, where did you get your clothes?" I smirked, knowing I had her, only I didn't. Far from it.

"Wow. They've really snowed everyone." A tense look took over her face and a definite show of pain was evident.

But before I could back pedal anything, she started. And for the first time in my fucking life, I literally felt like a piece of shit.

"Okay, we are doing this. Allow me to enlighten you. The last thing my parents—well my mom—bought for me was my first box of pads when I was twelve and a half because I stained the couch with my period one night while I had been asleep. Mind you, it was the first time I'd gotten my period and I had no clue what in the world was happening because she had never bothered to have that kind of talk with me. The only talk she had ever had with me was when I was ten and she told me, 'Don't you dare lay down for a man who can't afford a mansion and give you everything you've ever wanted. And if he wants a mistress or mistresses, you get on your knees and you make him happy regardless.'"

I saw more tears begin to assault her eyes, but Novalie continued. "I got beaten that morning for not knowing what was going on after I had put on that pad. The only time I ever got to eat was at school during the day, and occasionally when y'all have parties that are family-friendly." She inhaled breath after breath. Emotion was rolling off her in waves.

"Novalie, I had no idea . . ." And I really didn't. I wasn't trying to blow smoke up her ass and try to make myself look innocent, like I had seen so many others do in my lifetime.

"Ha!" She chuckled darkly. "None of y'all have had any clue because none of y'all have pulled your heads out your behinds and out of the MC to really check and see what's been going on. Did it ever occur to any of you to ask, where is Novalie? Is she okay? All the while my parents were gone on vacation to god knows where. And y'all are supposed to be all about family?"

Normally, I would've ripped her a new one for that attitude and for speaking to me like that. Only, a thought slammed into me like a damn brick. I didn't mind her attitude or her sass.

I felt Novalie's raw pain like it was in the air all around us.

"Then tell me, Novalie, how have you been keeping well? What happens when you've gotten sick?" That's what I really wanted to know.

"I've been keeping well because I've been working under the table at Virginia's diner in town. I've been paying the electricity bill. I've been buying myself clothes when I needed them. I've been buying the necessary items that a girl needs. Thankfully, they have been keeping the rent paid. And just for your information, luckily, the drug store around the corner doesn't look at identification when they make a sale. They know the issues and at least in their own messed up way, they're trying to help. Unlike some people." And with that, she left a lot unsaid.

"How much is that rent?" I asked, knowing good and damn well they haven't been paying that rent. As soon as French got his cut, they always took off.

"Four hundred seventy-five dollars. Why?" Just the cynical expression on her face at the mere mention of anyone asking about her parents appeared like it put a sour taste in her mouth.

"Well, fuck me." So that's where some of the club's funds have been disappearing too.

"What?" Her confused expression said it all.

"French hasn't been paying that rent. It's been on our expense sheets for years that the club has been paying. Since he's the Treasurer, we had him take care of all that." And with that, I whipped out my phone and sent out a massive wide text calling an emergency meeting in the morning.

Bright and god damn motherfucking early.

"Okay, so tell me, why have you stopped celebrating their anniversary on this date?"

Now, with the darkest chuckle of all, she knocked me clear on my ass when she stated, "Because their anniversary is November sixteenth, not May thirty-first."

Well, fuck me running. "Okay, then what the fuck are they in there celebrating for if today's date isn't their anniversary?"

"It's my birthday," she said with her head lowered.

"What the absolute fuck!" I roared out.

I was close to becoming unhinged. I was desperately trying to rein in the temper that was quickly overtaking my body. And just like all the other times—well, the few times I'd allowed my temper to be unleashed—people suffered. Sadly, it never went well for the individuals in my path, even the innocents.

"Then tell me, Novalie, how old are you today?" Because quite frankly, I had no god damn clue. And, another first in my life, I really felt like a fucking failure.

She was a part of my MC, my family. That bond should never have been broken, no matter the consequences. Even if their parent fucks up, the child still has their back watched always.

And it wasn't just me but the whole MC who just failed miserably.

"Eighteen today." God damn.

I really didn't want to know the answer to my next question, because it was going to show just how much of a failure I really was. "And when was the last time you celebrated your birthday?"

"My best friend, June, grabbed a cupcake for me at lunch when I was twelve. My parents had asked her mom if I could stay with them the night before because they were going on a cruise." She was starting to lose that fire I'd seen burning in her eyes earlier, and her voice was lowering.

"And the last time you got something simple as a damn gift?" This was another question I didn't want to know the answer to. What about Christmases? Where in the absolute fuck was the money that French-made and where the fuck were he and Amy always going?

Her lashes laid down on her pale cheeks.

Now, I really took the time to see her. Sure, she had cheekbones that were defined, always had been, but they were looking even more defined. Kind of like she hadn't been eating either a full meal or even three times a day for that matter.

"Umm . . . Cotton, I don't think I really want to share that with you." Her pale cheeks were now starting to change a hint toward light pink.

"Kitten, I'm not going to get angry, but I have to know the answer to my question." Yeah, I just called her Kitten. She had earned that nickname last night.

"Umm . . ." And now, those cheeks were a flaming red. Fucking cute. "Well, besides that cupcake, you mean?"

"Kitten, yeah." *What was she getting so embarrassed about*, I silently wondered.

"Well, besides that cupcake, a spa kit from the neighbor when I was fifteen, and that slice of cheesecake you gave me yesterday," she murmured.

I stood there so long gaping, I didn't even know how long, trying to make sure that I had in fact heard her right.

"Are you telling me . . . that . . . that you've only been given three things since you were twelve?" My voice was now at a low octave and I was barely hanging on by a thread.

"Yes," she whispered, and it was then that I realized it wasn't embarrassment painted all over her cheeks. No, it was nothing but sorrow, and one of the worst feelings in the world, shame.

I stormed over to a nearby table, picked it up, and threw it across the yard. Multiple shouts had come from inside and a few of my brothers had started to make their way out to me, but with a shake of my head, they all stayed put.

Once I had calmed down, I made my way back over to her, placing my finger under her chin and lifting it to face mine. "Open those baby blues for me, Kitten."

I waited for her to comply before I said another word. I wanted to make sure that she heard every word that was about to come from my mouth.

As soon as those baby blues were locked on my eyes from beneath those dark eyelashes, I started.

"Kitten. It. Is. Not. Your. Damn. Fault. Don't you ever blame yourself for their lacking ass bullshit. I'll be damned. Now, I'm going to take the blame as a whole with the MC. We should've seen what was happening and put an end to it." He ignored her visual protests and carried on. Heck, she even thought that placing her finger over his mouth, trying to tell him to stop, was going to keep him quiet. Fucking cute. "Now, and I mean starting now, you are going to take my number and keep it on you twenty-four-fucking-seven. No ifs ands or buts about it. You're also going to be getting a ride to and from school as well as to work and wherever else you want to go. What you are not going to do is keep anything else like this from me. I won't fucking have it. And you tell anyone who has a fucking problem with that, they have a problem with me."

It took a few minutes for everything I had said to sink in before she replied, "Okay, Cotton."

And thankfully, she didn't try to protest me. Nor did she try to argue with me. Perhaps she knew there was no winning that argument. For the vast majority, she looked like she was worn slap out. And no beautiful girl, no woman such as herself, should ever have to bear that look.

"Now, here's what we're going to do. We're going to go and get on my bike. We're going to ride to the diner, and you're going to have a slice of cake or a brownie or something, I don't rightly care."

I offered her my calloused hand, not taking no for an answer. And something told me, she would be the one to tell me no. And you want to know a secret? She would more than likely get away with it.

When Novalie placed her hand in mine, it was like an electric current flowed from her fingertips. It touched base with my palm, then radiated all the way to my heart and slammed home.

Instead of questioning that, I placed it on the back burner, because we had somewhere to be and I was too damn old for her.

As we left the backyard and rounded the building, I saw York, my Vice President, and called him over.

"You do not, and I mean you do not let French leave tonight before I get back and let you know. We're about to have a fucking intervention. And if that don't work, well, I'm bringing the shit to the table in the morning." I tried, but dammit all to hell, I couldn't keep the fury from my voice.

"Yeah, Pres. Hey, what's your name?" York asked Novalie with a smile, and it shocked the fuck out of me. Did people really not know who the fuck she was?

"Wow, guess dear old French and my mom really don't give a crap about me." I watched as she placed her free arm around her middle, and whether she realized it or not, she moved her body closer to mine and shut her face down to where she held a blank expression. I gave her a reassuring squeeze with my hand.

"Looks like that's part of the talk we're having in the morning?" Yeah, we were doing more than just talking with dear old French.

I didn't say any more as I steered Novalie and myself toward my bike. I had a 2012 Harley Dyna Glide. It was solid black with the Wrath MC logo painted on the gas tank, as all my brothers' bikes had as well.

When I climbed on, I handed her my helmet. No way was I going to have the only brain bucket I owned on my head, not while someone else was on my bike.

I knew I would end up getting her one. There was no way that shit was going to go on as it had. Over my dead body.

I was grateful that I didn't have to feel like a damn fucking cradle robber at finding out she was now eighteen.

As soon as she climbed on behind me, she wrapped her arms around my middle and held on.

It was then that I ran a few scenarios through my head and decided to choose Virginias's diner. This time of night it was one of the few places that was open twenty-four hours except on Sundays. On Saturdays they closed at two am on Sunday morning and didn't open back up until Monday morning at six in the morning.

It only took five minutes, but it felt like a lifetime. It always did on a bike.

"Virginia's?" she whispered and sent shivers up and down my body, which I chose to ignore. *You're too damn old for her*, I told myself silently. I was going to keep on reminding myself of that fact too.

"Well, I'll be damned if I'm going to let it pass that today is your birthday and no one got you something simple as a fucking cake."

I loved the way her lips lifted in a simple smile.

"I know you work here and shit but it's the only one open."

With that, we climbed off and made our way inside and to a back booth.

Virginia's Diner was what you'd expect it to be, even down to the black and white checkered floors and the solid red booths with the black marble tabletops.

Hell, she still had old soda fountains and a freeze machine from years past. Also, in one corner she had a couple pinball machines that every kid in the county tried to top the other.

A waitress came over to our booth. Since it was just them and two other couples in there, service was going to be quick.

"Want a milkshake, Kitten?" I was going to get fat tonight.

"Umm . . .."

"Hey, none of that shit. Do you want one?"

I saw her biting her bottom lip. Come on, darlin', where's that backbone that I know is there?

"Strawberry shake with a cherry, please?" she asked the waitress, but it was Novalie looking at me for confirmation that pissed me right the hell off.

Though not at her, never at her, at her situation with her fucked-up parents.

"Make that two and a slice of your molten chocolate lava cake and a slice of apple pie with vanilla ice cream," I ordered without looking at the waitress, whose name was Cindy. It wasn't the first time I had grabbed a bite here late at night. However, at those times, I never once saw Novalie on shift here.

I had my eyes on Novalie, watching her as she picked at her nails.

"Alright, be right out." I heard the seductive tone in her voice, but I wasn't in the mood to deal with that shit tonight.

"Thank you, Cotton." I saw Novalie wipe another tear from the corner of her eye.

Shit was definitely about to change.

"So, how's school?" I had to get her in a better mood. It was one thing for a girl, well, a woman to be upset, but it was another thing for someone who I was finding out fast had wiggled herself under my skin with a small conversation to be upset.

I didn't fucking like it.

Luckily, that sad expression she held on her face earlier seemed to ease as she talked.

"It's good. I take my SATs this Wednesday and if I do well on them, then hopefully, I'll hear back from some colleges I've applied to. I have graduation next Saturday."

"Yeah? Damn, that's good, Kitten. What you wanting to go to school for?" This was the most conversation that I had had with a female in a long fucking time. Especially one that didn't include taking her somewhere and fucking her until I was sated.

"Nursing school. Cliché, I know, but I want to be a NICU nurse. I want to have their backs as they fight in this world. Their bodies are so fragile, but dang it if they are not as strong or even stronger than me and you combined." That right there was one of the main reasons that I felt like a failure.

Someone who thought that way needed to be cherished and protected, not cast aside like they were nothing but yesterday's trash.

Before I spoke again, I had to reel in my anger so that it didn't transfer into my tone, "That's awesome, Kitten. How long would you go to school for?"

"Four years at a university would be ideal."

"There's a couple here in the state. You looking at them?"

"No, I have to get away from here. I have to find a better life for myself." The thought of her going away sickened me to my stomach.

"Well, I'm sure whatever you decide, you're going to kick ass." I smiled at her, one of a few smiles that came from me.

"Cotton, can I ask you something?" It was cute as fuck when she bit her bottom lip, something I noticed she did whenever she was nervous.

"Yeah, you can ask me just about anything." Well, anything that didn't involve the club.

"Cool." The light was back in Novalie's eyes like it had been when I'd handed her that slice of cheesecake. "Why do you call me Kitten?"

"To be honest, the other day, you were riled like a little kitten and you went out with your claws bared. Plus, you're cute like a kitten." With that, I felt like a damn teenager who hadn't yet hit puberty.

And then, boom, it happened—her cheeks got pink again. Fucking. Cute.

Before she could make a comeback, the waitress was back with their shakes, pie, and cake.

"Anything else I can get for you?" She hadn't asked us, only me.

"No. And don't come back until we're ready to leave." I emphasized the 'we', knowing good and damn well it wasn't going to phase her of all people because it never did, but at least I made the effort.

"Well, there goes your figure," Novalie murmured as I put my fork into my slice of pie.

"Fucking funny," I chuckled. There was that comeback I was waiting for. "I am not going to sing you "Happy Birthday", so just pretend there's a candle and make a wish."

Damn, but I wished she was older. I loved it when her eyes sparkled like they had just done.

"Thank you, Cotton. Really."

We sat there for another hour or so talking. She told me about the times for her SATs and that her mom was supposed to be picking her up and then we talked about her graduation.

It was nearing the end of the night when I told her I wanted her to call me if she needed me. In fact, I made her promise.

"Okay, Cotton, but I'll have to borrow someone else's phone. I don't have the money right now for a phone." And when she said that, I wanted to pummel French's face in.

She was a young woman. What was she supposed to do if she ever got into trouble and needed someone? Fucking let them hurt her? Not on my goddamn watch.

I wasn't sure how long I sat there quietly stewing over that fact until I felt a gentle hand atop mine and it broke me out of my dark mood.

Then she said my name with a tenderness in her tone. "Cotton?"

"I'm fine, Kitten. You ready?"

"Yeah."

I signaled for the waitress, took out a few bills for our meal, and handed them to her. "Keep the change," I murmured. It wasn't that she was a good waitress—she wasn't—but every little bit helped.

When I accepted the original ticket, I saw a number written on the bottom of it. It didn't escape Novalie's notice either as I saw her let out a little huff and roll her eyes.

I crumpled the ticket and then threw it in one of our glasses. I was going to do this anyway, not because of Novalie but because I had to do it quite frequently. I never dipped where I lived, and that was a rule that I lived by. I placed my hand on the small of her back and led her from the diner.

As I pulled my bike into her driveway, I helped her off and chuckled when the helmet strap got stuck.

"Anytime you need me, Kitten, you call me. I don't care what time of day it is, you fucking call me. I'll have a phone to you tomorrow morning. I'll program my cell and the club's phone number in it. You can't get me on either one, then you blow up both phones until you can. Now, there may be a case where I cannot be disturbed, and this is only for emergencies, otherwise, I'll call you back. Give me a code word that you'll give me, so I know I need to drop whatever it is and get to you, yeah?"

"Umm . . . unicorn," she said abashedly.

Fucking cute.

With a small lift of my mouth, I shook my head as I looked down. Damn when was the last time I had actually really fucking smiled?

"Unicorn it is then." Never in my wildest dreams did I think a woman would ever give me 'unicorn' as a safe word. A thirty-five-year-old man being told by an eighteen-year-old woman that her safe word was unicorn . . . damn.

"Thank you, Cotton. Thank you for actually caring." Then she did something that knocked me on my ass yet again—she kissed my cheek. Her lips were soft against my skin, a softness that I've never felt before. I knew in that moment that I would do whatever I needed to, to make sure that softness never escaped her.

"Kane. I'm never Cotton to you, or Pres. I'm Kane."

"Cotton, I—"

"No, babe. Kane. I'm Kane to you and to you alone." I had no god damn idea where that had come from, but I needed this like I needed fucking air.

"Okay. Well, goodnight, Kane." As soon as my name came from her mouth, I felt warm all over. Everything in my body felt like liquid fire.

"Night, Kitten," I whispered into the night air.

I sat on my bike and waited for her to get inside and lock her door. While I'd been waiting, I made plans.

One of those plans was getting another seat for her on my bike. That little ass pad had to be uncomfortable, but not once did she complain.

With that, I backed out, revved up my Harley, and headed to the clubhouse to make some damn heads roll.

Shit was about to take a turn for Novalie, whether she fucking liked it or not.

I was going to get her squared away and then I was going to stay in the shadows and be the one person who would have her back no matter what.

Chapter 2

'Why do trucks put big tires on the front and smaller ones on the back? Freaking weird.'

Novalie

Come Saturday morning, I laid in my bed and ran last night's events through my mind. It was so random and yet so perfect. That had been the best birthday that I'd ever had in my entire life. Heck, if I were being honest, that night was the best day of my whole life so far.

I still chuckled when Cotton had told me that he wasn't singing "Happy Birthday" to me but still told me to make a wish without the candle.

Even more so when he had asked me to call him Kane, and that was for myself, alone.

Feeling like an emotional cow, I shook myself out of my reverie and reminded myself that it was friends and friends only. I had to remind myself to never, ever let it cross that line.

I knew that I had nothing on the girls who hung around the club and some of the women I had seen hanging all over Cotton when he let them.

Well, maybe the women hanging all over him was an overstretch. The most he ever really allowed them to do was touch his arm animatedly when they were talking, and that was it.

I lost count of the number of times he pushed women off of him and the amount of times his brothers had pushed women back.

Not to mention I had heard way too many of the club girls either bragging about the fact they were going to be the one to tame Cotton and be the woman on his arm. Or they were complaining about the fact that he didn't let them touch him, only he was allowed to touch them, and he always did them from behind.

At the time that had been mentioned in the clubhouse, I had no idea what that really meant. I had only been thirteen at the time. Lucy, one of the ole' ladies who actually gave a damn, was looking after me some. She wasn't mad that I'd heard any of that. No, she was spitting mad at the fact the club girls thought that it had been okay to be talking about Cotton behind his back.

I didn't know if Lucy ever told him, but there were no more talks about Cotton in or out of the clubhouse. Then I'd found out that some of the women who had been bragging were no longer club girls.

It was said that they rotated them out every year, however a few of the girls had been there for going on three years or more.

It wasn't that we lived closed off from the rest of humanity. Nor was it just the fact that we lived in a small town. A lot of it had to do with the simple fact that the world we lived in was on the outside of normal and the life in an MC.

And in Clearwater, North Carolina, a rural town, the MC was the biggest talk of the town. Even though they did a lot for their community and for the state as a whole. It was said that the members of the community hated them. Which was freaking stupid if you asked me.

But they didn't hate that they also had the best garage in three counties and people from all over came to them to get mechanic work.

People who looked in from the outside thought the worst of the members because they didn't understand that world. But once you're in, nine times out of ten you don't ever want to leave.

It wasn't that I wanted to leave the MC. It was that I wanted to get away from my parents and this small town. I only had three friends. Three? How crazy is that?

I had June, but for some reason she hadn't been around lately. I also had Cree when we were at the parties, but the age gap is rough. And last but not least, Virginia.

But now, I guessed in a way I also had Cotton on my side.

Clearing my mind yet again from those thoughts, I looked at the clock and realized I had to be at work in two hours.

After I showered, I'd demolished a bowl of cereal, which was my regular meal because it was cheap.

It had been while I was getting ready for my shift that there was a knock on the front door.

When I went to it, I looked out the peephole, I saw one of the prospects I recognized as Xavier.

"Morning," I said. Xavier wasn't anywhere near as tall as Cotton, with him being six-foot-two and Xavier being more like five-foot-eleven. I was still short compared to them all with my five-foot-three-inch frame.

"Morning, Miss. Novalie. This is from the Pres. Hope you have a good one," Xavier stated as he stood in my open doorway.

I looked at the crimson-colored gift bag. Again, I reiterated to myself, a crimson-colored bag. When Cotton had asked me what my favorite color was, after he disclosed that his was red, I'd told him mine was crimson.

When he asked me why that color, I had told him that while, yes, I was a Carolina girl, I pulled for Alabama.

"Umm, it's crimson," I murmured, then realized that I said it aloud, my cheeks I was sure had to be sporting a light pink color.

"Well, I don't know all that went on when the Pres returned late last night, but he went on a tear. I could even hear them from behind the doors while they were in church."

"Everyone okay?" I hoped that he hadn't gone on a tear because of me. I didn't want anyone to get harmed.

"I reckon. But you have a good day." With that, he turned and walked to his bike.

When I closed and locked the door, I took the bag to the kitchen table and then peered at the contents inside.

I saw a few different boxes and some things, but first I picked up the card that had my name written in a manly script, almost unreadable. And as I opened it, three hundred-dollar bills fell to the floor.

> 'Kitten, happy late birthday. Wasn't much I could do last night. But I hope this helps.' - Kane

With everything that he'd already done, I wanted to ring his neck. I even pinched myself on my arm to make sure I wasn't dreaming before I got too carried away.

The first thing I picked up was a gift card to my favorite bookstore in town. I had told him that I loved books last night, as if it hadn't already been obvious.

Next, there was a bag of my favorite candies, peanut butter m&m's.

Then, I picked up the unwrapped black box. Inside was the sleekest-looking phone I'd ever seen. It looked just like June's phone, and I knew that phone was one of the newest and fanciest on the market.

When I turned the phone on, I saw it had a full battery, and on a sticky note on the side of the box was my number.

The screen that popped up was a photo of Cotton's Harley. The cocky weirdo, I was smiling so wide that my cheeks were starting to hurt but I didn't care, not in the slightest. And on my home screen was a text message. I wasn't tech-savvy—this was my first ever cell phone after all.

But thanks to June, I at least knew the basics. This was going to be entertaining.

The name wasn't listed as Cotton in my contacts. It was Kane.

Kane - If you're reading this, this is your new phone.

So, I clicked at the bottom and finger pecked, grinning to myself that I was texting Cotton. But this was all too much.

Novalie - Thank you, Kane. But this is just too much. I really can't accept any of this.

Kane - The fuck it is. It isn't nowhere near enough.

I couldn't even imagine the tone of voice that he would've used when he said that.

Kane - Don't you dare think you're giving any of it back. I'll tan your hide.

Tan my hide? What did he . . . then it hit me. Would he really spank me? And then I closed that door on that thought.

Since I could already feel that friend's line being crossed. That was so not happening.

Novalie - Still Kane this is too much, but okay. Thank you.

Any other time I would have argued with him, but this was the first time that someone had really put thought into something for me.

Kane - Welcome. Get to work. Have a good shift. Don't forget your promise.

And as I walked out of the house, there sat York in a car waiting to take me to work.

We didn't talk the rest of that day until I was locking my door and a beep sounded from my new phone.

Kane - You make it home okay?

It was almost as if he had someone watching me. And just how had he known what time I had to be at work that morning? That was just Cotton.

Novalie - Yes. Just locked the door.

Kane - Okay. Night.

Novalie - Night Kane

However, every morning since Sunday, I had a morning message from Cotton that I replied back to. And a good night message that I most definitely replied back to as well.

We had also texted a little on Tuesday when I'd been seeing the same bike following me everywhere. When he had explained that he was not failing me again, that had started a heated conversation, which he won because he wasn't giving me that.

And then come Wednesday, I woke up early and got ready, then I jumped in June's Jeep and went to take my SATs and ace that heifer.

***

Sitting on the steps of the school wasn't something new. Since eleven in the morning, I had been staring at my watch as the minutes ticked on past three in the afternoon, knowing deep down that my mother had forgotten about me yet again.

I regretted what I was about to do. I despised asking for help, but I was tired of trusting in the fact that maybe, just maybe, one day my mom was actually going to put me first and not her husband nor the drugs I knew her to be taking.

French hated the fact that I wasn't his daughter, which he made known every time I was in his presence, though let's face it, that wasn't all that often anymore.

Even more so the fact that my mother had gotten her tubes tied after she had me. She didn't reveal that fact to French until after she had him wrapped around her little pinky. And sadly, he didn't take that out on my mom, he took that out on me, as if it was all my fault.

Sighing, I grabbed my phone, which now, due to a promise that I'd made to Cotton that I would call him if I ever needed him, had gone with me everywhere. I hadn't really expected Cotton to give me a phone, but he did. And for one of the first times in my life, someone had kept their promise to me.

Taking a deep breath, I called Cotton.

On the second ring, he answered.

"Yeah." He sounded hurried. "Hold the fuck on!" I heard roared into the phone after I heard a lot of background noise.

"Kane, is this a bad time?" Dang it.

"What? No, Kitten, what is it? Everything okay?" And all the noises that I heard suddenly ceased.

"Yeah, just that . . ." God, I hated interrupting anyone, most of all him.

Softening his voice, "Kitten, spit it out, yeah? What is it?"

"She forgot again. Can you pick me up at school?" I asked with my eyes closed, wishing for the ground to just swallow me whole.

"I'm going to fucking strangle her." he growled.

"Kane . . ."

"Kitten, I'll be there in five." With that, he hung up.

Sadly, while I had been waiting, memories began assaulting me when I was younger. I still held something from Cotton, and I haven't breathed a word of what all really happened to me between the years of six and twelve. I wasn't ever going to tell him, not if I could help it.

I lost count how many teachers tried to get social services after my mother, however none of it worked. Somehow my mother found out when social services were coming to the house to check the conditions.

It was only then I got secondhand clothes that actually fit, shoes, a clean house, and hot water.

But as soon as the officers left, things went right back to how they used to be.

And for the first time in my entire life, someone said they would be somewhere for me, and they were. It took Cotton four minutes forty-five seconds to come rolling up on his Harley.

I smiled when I saw him. Only a few other students and some teachers were hanging around the front of the school, and all of them stopped what they were doing and watched as he pulled his Harley right in front of the steps, so close in fact that our fingertips could touch.

Then I watched, just as the other students and teachers stared in awe as Cotton took off his helmet and his long hair fell around his shoulders.

I may have just turned eighteen and I may be innocent as a young babe, but I read romance books. I knew the ins and outs, and that man, yes, he was old enough to be my father, but try as I might, I just couldn't see him in that kind of light.

I also knew that no way did I have a chance in hell with the man, but I would always settle for being his friend.

"Kitten, you ready?" he asked me as he pulled a second helmet from his saddle bag and handed it to me. I noticed that it had some crimson accents on it.

A sudden jolt of electricity wrapped me in waves as our fingertips touched.

"Yeah," I said as I stood up and grabbed my bag. "Thanks for coming." I had a small smile on my face, one that I knew was going to be only for Cotton.

There were so many layers to this man.

"I got you. Always," he said matter-of-factly with a tip of his eyebrow. What I had noticed was that all the people outside of the school stood stock-still and a few of them even had their mouths hanging wide open.

Only, what stopped my mind from processing anything else was the fact that I hadn't seen him looking at anyone but me.

"You remember what I told you on Saturday?" And just like that, I was focused once again on this man.

"Yeah, I remember." With glee in my voice, I climbed on behind him, placed my tennis shoe-covered feet on the pegs as I wrapped my arms around his waist.

"Good. Hold on, Kitten." I couldn't contain the laughter.

I loved the thrill. It was magnificent. And I hoped this wouldn't be the last time that I got to be on the back of his bike.

Yes, it was only a few minutes being on the back of the bike, but it was precious to me and it was free. There was no other feeling on Earth quite like it. If I ever found a sensation that was even similar to it, then that would be on my top favorite everything in the world. We had been about a block from the clubhouse when Cotton stopped suddenly in the middle of the road.

"Kitten, tuck your head down and put your face in my shoulder blades." His tone allowed no room for an argument, so I did as he said.

My breathing sped up, ratcheting up to a hundred when I saw Cotton's hand reach for something in the back of his jeans. When I saw his hand curl around it, I knew exactly what it was—a gun.

Then a warm sensation flooded me, I knew that no matter what, Cotton wouldn't let any harm come to me. How did I know that? It was never said to me, but that was Cotton. His actions proved everything.

"Cotton," I heard a man's voice say with a light rasp.

I felt Cotton tighten his frame to rock hard beneath my hands. His front was coiled and ready to strike should he need to. But no sounds came from his mouth.

"Need to have a meet," the same voice stated.

"Negative," Cotton responded with no emotion in his voice. *How did he do that*, I wondered. How could he be that serious at times?

"Look, I can make real big problems for you," that voice rasped out, I knew that was the wrong thing for the man to stay.

"You think you can threaten me in my town? You fucking blind? Motherfucker, you got no clue who you're talking to like that," Cotton rumbled out. I wouldn't want to be on the other side of his temperament.

"Know you got a sweet little piece of ass sitting on the back of your bike. Also know she means something to the club, not just to you." I flinched at the words that came from the man's mouth. Cotton's other hand came down to my thigh and squeezed, almost as if telling me without words that it was going to be alright, that he had my back. While I had been looking down, I saw Cotton tightening his hand around his gun.

"We'll plan a meet." And with that, Cotton gunned his engine and left the man in the middle of the street.

Thankfully, I didn't hear any passersby.

We drove to the clubhouse and he parked his bike in his spot next to the long line of bikes.

"Kitten, that helmet stays with this bike for you and you alone." That wonderful feeling crept through my whole body yet again.

God, I was so confused. Yes, he had proven with just the smallest of actions that he would be there no matter what if I needed him.

But it was the small things that he was doing, like the helmet and buying me a phone and that candy, with it all packed into a gift bag of my favorite color and hand-delivered to me. Not to mention, where I sat that night on his bike on my birthday, had been a little uncomfortable, but this time, he had a different seat on the back of his bike.

"Okay, Kane. Thanks." I still felt weird calling him Kane and not Cotton. Maybe it was that I hadn't heard anyone else calling him Kane.

And right after I got the helmet off, Cotton said something that rocked my whole world.

"Kitten, need you to know, the only thing that kept me from blowing a hole in that fucker's brain was the fact that had I done that, then you would've been put on their radar a lot worse than what you are now. I got no damn clue where he's coming from, but I'm going to find out. Top of that, had I reacted any other way, others would've seen and they would know I've got a weakness. Now, I've got some things to take care of, then I'll take you home. Yeah?"

"Cool" was all I knew to say. And then I threw caution to the wind and hugged him. "Thanks again, Kane." He wrapped one arm around me, squeezed me closer to his body, kissed the crown of my head, then he let go.

From his speech, what I got was that I was his weakness. And that was a foreign feeling that before now would have been totally unwelcomed by me. Now, though, I had someone in my corner.

I knew then and there that there was nothing that I wouldn't do, if Cotton asked it of me. If he'd asked me to jump, I would've asked how high.

Then, I spotted Cree and made my way over.

While we talked, Cree mentioned she was still struggling with her schoolwork. And she told me that in some of the classes, the students picked on her and bullied her because she didn't have a mother and she was raised by a bunch of bikers. She said that a lot of them called her a club slut.

I had asked her if she had mentioned any of this to her dad, but she vehemently shook her head. Cree said that none of this was her dad's fault. It wasn't his fault that the woman who gave birth to her was a junkie whore, and it wasn't her dad's fault that life had dealt him the cards it had. She took up for her dad in every way humanly possible.

To steer the conversation away from bad memories that I could see written all over Cree's face, her eyes hooded over and looking so beaten down, I asked if she knew of any shops that had good discounts on clothing. Cree's face lit up and we made plans to hit one of the neighboring towns for a girls' day out, something that I had never done in my entire life. The last time I went shopping for clothes was about a year ago, and that was at a local thrift store. I had other important matters to see to with my money and having electricity and hot water had been high on my list. I had grown accustomed to hot showers.

After a few hours, Cotton took me home and with the same goodnight as before, but he had added a kiss on my forehead. He waited until I locked the front door before he left.

I swore I was never going to wash my forehead again. But just my luck, that night when I'd taken a shower, from where I had massaged my scalp, the shampoo flowed onto my forehead.

***

My time at the clubhouse was always the same, me skating by with no one saying a word to me, except sometimes Cree, Garret, Lucy, and Cotton. Always Cotton. Yes, it was one word here and there, but it was the thought that counted to me.

But the moment I'd walked through the main door of the clubhouse behind Cotton today, all eyes and heads had turned to me, and instantly, "Hey, Novalie" had sounded all throughout the clubhouse.

It had scared me to the point that I had instinctively gathered closer to Cotton.

"It's okay, Kitten. This club came to an understanding." I knew that was more than likely all that I was going to get on the matter. Not to mention Xavier had told me that Cotton had gone on a tear.

To be honest, I knew most of their names since all I had ever done was sat in the shadows and observed, but I shocked the heck out of them when I said hey to all of them and had asked each one of them a question about their lives that I had heard in passing, just to show that even though they hadn't cared to get to know me, I had tried to get to know them.

And when I had finished and looked over my shoulder, Cotton had been standing in the doorway observing. I caught the barest hint of a smile before he walked away to where I figured was his office.

That night, a dozen images assaulted me of a life that I'd only ever dreamed about. What were the odds that I would have dreams that would turn into a reality? I was no match for the kind of woman Cotton needed.

So, I resigned myself to find a man like him. He had already shown me that a few acts of kindness went a long way. If there was a man out there like him, I was bound and determined to find him.

I never told anyone what the kids at school thought of me. It wasn't just Cree who they said those things about. Cree had someone to go to and tell, I just simply didn't. And even if I did, I highly doubted that I would tell anyone.

I had just drifted off to sleep when a sound woke me. Bleary-eyed and my head fuzzy, I looked around and tried to figure out what that sound had been.

After a few moments, I heard it again, only it sounded like glass was being shattered followed by what sounded like it was being stepped on.

Kicking into overdrive as my breath hitched, I grabbed my cell, unplugged it from the charger, and called Cotton.

And when it rang and rang and rang and then went to voicemail, I called the clubhouse like he told me to do. If any time warranted trying to get ahold of him, this definitely did.

On the second ring, someone answered, "Yeah?"

In a low voice, I spoke out as fast as I could. "This is Novalie. I need to speak to Kane." I shivered at the sounds that I now heard. The floorboards were creaking.

Creaking almost to the point of them sounding like nails being grated against a chalkboard.

"Novalie, there's no one named Kane here. You call the right number?" Xavier asked me.

"Cotton, Xavier. I need to talk to Cotton. It's important. Now." The creaking of the floorboards was getting louder.

"Ah, well, he's in church, girl. You know I can't interrupt them. I'll take a message for you, but I'm sorry." He didn't really sound sorry. Heck, I didn't blame him. I knew to never interrupt the members while that particular door was closed.

If at any point and time that door was open, you could go in, but again, that was a big if.

"This is an emergency, Xavier. Please."

"Doesn't matter, Novalie. He can't be disturbed." Oh, come on, prospect.

"Xavier, tell him 'unicorn'. Please, Xavier. Please." I could feel the tears welling in my eyes.

Either it was the shakiness in my voice or the sound of fear that I knew had to have shown through, he murmured, "Unicorn? Fuck. Hang on. Fuck. Shit. There goes my damn patch."

A few minutes later, I heard mumbling and yelling even though the speaker piece had been shoved into a shirt or something because the sounds were so muffled. I decided that I was going to ask for Xavier to not be in trouble.

And the moment I heard Cotton's voice through the phone, it took all I had to not break down in tears. How much did fate think I could handle?

"Kitten?" Cotton would come, of that I had no doubt.

All I had to do was listen and stay safe. I ran into my closet and tried to make myself as small as I could behind an old quilt.

However, that all went to hell in a handbasket. I thought I'd been quiet, but not quiet enough apparently, because I felt a hand grab hold of my hair and yank my head back with my body following suit.

Chapter 3

'Every Beast needs His Beauty.'

Cotton

The Sunday after her birthday I had laid it out for French, "French, I don't give a goddamn if she is or isn't your daughter. When you married her mom, she became yours. Yours to love, yours to protect, yours to have her god damn back. And you've fucking failed. Fuck, I can't even count the times you've fucking failed her!"

"Cotton . . ." French started. I was already sick of looking at him.

"Don't you dare Cotton me, you son of a bitch. Fucking pathetic the shit you and Amy have been pulling. One more damn time you let Novalie down, I swear, you will be done with this club. And there won't be a rock big enough you can hide under."

"You going to throw me out because of something that little bitch said . . ." Before I knew it, I was out of my chair and halfway across the room, losing my temper.

I didn't give French another minute to say a word before I pulled my fist back and punched him with one solid hit. It wasn't hard enough to do any damage, but damn, I got my point across. If French hadn't been in the booze, that punch would've only staggered him back, not knocked him to the damn ground as it did.

"You ever disrespect her again in front of me, I'll lay your god damn ass out. And if y'all let her down, that includes your," I emphasized 'your', "ole' lady as well, I'll strip you of your damn patch so fast it'll make your head spin." I was so damn pissed off. Given just the few tidbits of information that Novalie had shared, who wouldn't be pissed off for her?

"Now, get your ass out of my clubhouse and do your damn job. We've got bikes out the ass that need work. And you better step up for Novalie," I told him as he had been sitting on his ass drinking a beer instead of actually doing the club any favors.

I saw the fucker getting ready to snarl in my direction, but he wisely thought better of it.

So, I pulled my phone out and texted Novalie.

Cotton – Let me know if French or your mom talks to you today.

Kitten – Okay. Is everything okay?

Cotton – It will be.

On Wednesday after I had dropped her off at her house from picking her up at school, I called church, as they all filed in one by one, I noticed French had yet to show. I also noticed that Novalie hadn't said whether either one of them had talked to her today.

Once the door closed, I slammed the gavel down and church was in session.

"Look, I know it takes a lot for us to kick out a member of this club. To be honest, we've never had to do it before. As you all know, the shit with Novalie is fucked the fuck up. That girl never should've been put in the position she was put in. Not to mention the simple fact that none of us really knew what was going on, and that's something that should've never happened. I've also been noticing a few issues with the cash flow and the accounting. I had Dale take a look at the numbers and the cameras." I allowed all of that to sink in.

Not one of my brothers even seemed surprised. I didn't know if that was a good thing or a very bad thing.

"Dale, what did you find?" I opened the floor to him. If information was out there, then Dale could find it.

"First of all, Cotton had me look into the books for the past six months. It wasn't obvious—matter of fact, if someone didn't know what they were looking for, it all would've looked above board. French has been using the club for his personal cash cow to fund his little adventures. Totaling it all up, it came to over a hundred grand." Every member of the club looked surprised, then you could feel the fury coming off of them in waves.

"Third, I found another irregularity. I did some digging into it and it seems that he's been giving some of that money to another MC." Rounds of furious words stormed from my brothers' mouths.

"Don't you dare tell me it's the Spades MC. Especially seeing as they've been trying to take over our pipeline." That came from the club's Enforcer, Garret.

If that came out of Dale's mouth. French's time here was done. Club vote be damned.

"Then I guess I don't need to say it," Dale said with anger written all over his face.

"Fuck! What the fuck? First, he's paying the Spades our damn money. And then their President thinks that it's okay to have words with Cotton. And then, he made comments about Novalie. Shit ain't fucking right," Knox said with a snarl and the fact that he had said all of that at once, that wasn't something to be taken lightly. Multiple words of agreements were shouted out around the table.

"Y'all ain't going to like this either, but I took a look at the cameras. Sometimes when we've been out, a figure has been seen going into your office, Pres. A figure that looks a lot like Amy. She's always covered, but that tattoo on her right hand is always visible. It can be seen plain as day."

That tattoo being a four-leaf clover between her index finger and thumb.

"I don't think I need to do this, but it's club law. Anyone opposed to French leaving the club, say 'aye'." And I waited, but not a sound came from anyone.

"Anyone opposed to French staying in the club, say 'aye'." And it was before I got the aye out of my own mouth that the room erupted in ayes. With that, I pounded the gavel on the table.

"We'll have to find them again and take a trip." That was a trip I was looking forward to. The notion of stripping one of my brothers from my club, a club that I'd started eighteen years ago, didn't sit well with me. But avenging the club, yeah, that sat well with me. I had selected the first officers. French wasn't the first generation of officers, like Cooper, York, and Garret, but he was still one of my selected brothers. If I wouldn't have brought the vote to the table, then my brothers never would have even considered voting French in. However, had I not brought the vote to the table, then I never would've met my Kitten.

I gave the man a chance though. I had seen him standing on a corner with a sign and a tin can. Gave him a warm place to sleep, food on the table, and money in his pocket, and this is how he repays that trust?

A knock sounded on the door, I was about to go off the rails at whomever was at that door. Everyone knew to never interrupt us while those doors were closed. It was one of our most sacred laws that was never to be broken.

The prospect poked his head in, I was about to have that prospect's kutte stripped from his back.

"Prospect—" I started but the pale look on the otherwise tanned man made me pause.

"Look, Cotton, I mean Pres, I think you need to take this call." Hell, the boy looked like he was about to shit his pants.

"Boy, you been a prospect for almost two fucking years. You fucking know better!" York yelled from across the room.

All the other brothers slapped their fists on the table in agreement.

"I . . . I know . . . but Pres, Novalie called in and asked for Kane. There's no one here by that name, and then she said you and told me to tell you a word . . ." Only one person on this planet had the right to call me Kane. Only one. And it was then that a few of my brothers gave me unrecognizable looks.

"Who's Kane?" A few of the other brothers rumbled that same question around the table.

"Get on with it, fucker!" Cooper stated at my left.

"Unicorn." That was the last word I wanted to hear.

"Phone, now," I snapped.

I went from postal to an eerie calm that signaled I was about to rip someone's head off. That was our safe word.

Even the temperature in the room seemed to be in a deep chill. I felt all their eyes on me. No one knew my given name but a few of the officers, more like two. It was the looks from my other brothers that had changed. They'd been on the fence about Novalie, since some of them had never taken the time to even learn her name. Now, I guessed that was all different.

But what I did know was that Novalie had just gotten all of my brothers' respect. The fact that I allowed her to interrupt me in church said it all.

When I put the phone to my ear, I could hear Novalie's heavy breathing. Something was wrong, especially since she used our safe word. Any other time, had someone said the word 'unicorn', I would've thought they were off their rocker.

"Kitten?" I could hear it in my own voice. Worry.

I didn't notice the eyebrow lifts from my brothers at the table.

"Kane?" Her whisper was strained. I could even hear the cracks in her voice, and I guessed she was close to tears, if not already crying.

"I'm here, Kitten, what is it?" I ignored all the looks of wonder when the word 'kitten' came from my mouth the second time, and I didn't give a shit if they saw the raw vulnerability that was there. If a man wouldn't allow himself to be seen vulnerable when he was with the ones he trusted the most, then he wasn't really a man.

"There . . . there's someone in the house," she whispered, and I could tell through the phone that she was scared out of her mind.

My blood turned to ice.

Without telling my brothers anything in church, I stormed out of my chair at the head of the table, hearing it knock back against the wall as I flung the door the rest of the way open and ran to my truck.

Normally, I hated being in a cage, but this was the last straw. She was getting her shit and moving in with me.

He made her a promise, and I would be damned if I'd be another notch in a long line of people who have let her down.

Thankfully the line for the clubhouse went to a burner phone so none of the calls could be traced.

"Kitten, get into your closet and cover yourself up as best you can. Don't make a fucking sound, Kitten. Leave your phone on. I'm coming," I told her as I fired up my truck, standing on the throttle as my passenger door was yanked open and York climbed inside.

Without waiting for him to fully close the door, we sped out of the main lot.

I heard my brothers' bikes tearing down the road right behind us. At least most of them, if not all of them, were following in pursuit. Fifteen bikers.

I never, and I meant I never, stormed out of church for anything. Nor were you supposed to ever bring a phone inside of church. But when the prospect said Novalie was on the phone and had used our safe word, that was a game-changer.

"Kitten, don't talk, just listen. I'm five minutes out. Keep quiet as best you can," I ordered as I put the phone on speaker.

"Call French and find out where the fuck he is," I stealthily whispered at York, not wanting for whomever was in the house to hear me on the phone.

"Yeah, fuck." I noticed York shaking his head as he then spoke, "Look, man, first you need to have your goddamned phone on. Second, you need to call Cotton, and third, you need to get home and handle your shit. Mainly your god damn daughter, you piece of shit." York's temple was throbbing from how pissed off he was. Though none of them were as pissed off as I was.

I had thought that when we had that talk the morning after their so-called anniversary party, that I had gotten through to both of them. Obviously not.

"Get a couple of the boys rounded up for a little trip tomorrow. Call Dale. I want a location on French. I don't give a god damn how he has to go about it. You get that damn location."

"Fucking A," York said as he placed a call to Dale. Dale didn't drive at night because his vision was shit, so I knew that he hadn't been one of the brothers behind us.

I pressed down on the accelerator, weaving in and out of the last stretch of traffic.

When we made it to her house, I saw the truck that was parked haphazardly in her drive.

Without my truck being fully stopped, I hauled ass to the front door, yelling at York. "York, take a look in that fucking truck." Then I made my way into the house with my gun in my hand.

With the phone off speaker and now pressed to my ear, I spoke as softly and as quietly as I could.

"Kitten, which bedroom?"

I heard her yip out and then she said, "Stairs. Last door on the—"

I heard a scream pierce through the house, a blood-curdling scream, and I noticed the shattered glass on the living room floor. Fucking amateur, thank fuck.

I bounded my way up the stairs, taking two at a time with my gun at the ready. When I rounded the corner, I saw the son of a bitch with her hair wrapped in his fist.

"Telling you now, I'm getting mine before that bitch gets a hold of you," he snarled at my Kitten. Wrong move, motherfucker.

And before either the man or my Kitten could react, I popped off a shot and hit that asshole in the shoulder of the arm that had held her hair. Instantaneously, he let go of her hair and whirled around.

"Oh fuck." The man went pale and wide-eyed as soon as he realized who exactly was standing at the door.

I took a moment and looked over Novalie, making sure that not one bruise started to form.

Novalie didn't hesitate as she hauled her ass to me. I wrapped my free arm around her and pulled her tight to my body. Leaning down, I placed a kiss on the crown of her head.

"You okay, Kitten?" I whispered in her hair with my eyes trained on the man who was holding the wound in his shoulder.

"Yes, Kane," she whispered. I could feel her body trembling with fright.

It was loud enough for York and the slimy fuck, Frankie, to hear, and Frankie heard the fact that she had the right to call me something other than Cotton. The man pissed himself and didn't even try to run away or hide that fact.

My brothers entered the room and I watched as Garret hauled the son of a bitch out.

"Kitten, you're not safe here," I said after I holstered my gun and wrapped my other arm around her too.

"I want you to pack everything you have. You're done staying here. You're staying with me." That last part?

What the fuck was that? But it would seem that my heart was leading my body and not my head. Damn emotions could walk out the door. But to be honest I liked the idea of being around her more. I wasn't close to a lot of people, and I wouldn't mind being more than a protector for her, possibly even going so far as having her for a friend. It was the least I knew I would get.

I was just too old for her to have anything more.

"And put this on," I told her as I took off my kutte, shucked out of my hoodie, and handed it to her then replaced my kutte.

The damn hoodie fell to just above her knees. I knew she was tiny, but that put it all into perspective.

"Okay, Kane." I stood sentry in her door as I watched her grab a duffle from the bottom of her closet and fill it with the things hanging in her closet as well as a shoebox from the top of her closet.

Fuck, but the state of the house even pissed me off. There had been no furniture in the living room, though the floors looked clean, and there had been no pictures on the walls. In her bedroom, she slept on a mattress. One fucking mattress. She had a milk crate for a nightstand, and I didn't even see a damn dresser, but I did see one cardboard box that housed her clothes that wouldn't hang.

"Kitten, where's the rest of your stuff?" I asked her, hoping like all get out that she had more than that.

"This is it, Kane. It's been just me." She looked at me, and I hated that I had even asked her that now.

"No worries. I'll rectify all of this shit." Damn, I felt like a fucking failure all over again. When would all the blows end?

"Ready, Kane." She grabbed her duffle, but I was there before she grabbed it fully. And the cardboard box. The only thing I let her carry was the shoebox and she seemed to have a death grip on that.

"Okay, Kitten. Let's go."

I headed down the stairs in front of her. None of my brothers were getting a look at what she had on either—a damn threadbare t-shirt that showed too much skin for my comfort and fucking tight ass panties that showed off her well-rounded ass. Thank fuck for that hoodie. I had to imagine someone's flesh being pulled from their body to keep from getting hard.

It was as we were exiting the house that I saw half my brothers were waiting at the front door for us. And all with a raving Frankie in our club van that mysteriously happened to be there as well. Hell, I could hear the man whining and begging to be released. Shit wasn't going to happen

"Telling y'all fuckers now, keep your god damn eyes to your fucking selves," I growled out.

I ignored all their smirks and soft chuckles, knowing they would all respect what I said, and they would show her the respect she deserved.

They were damn sure not seeing her in what she had on. Thank fuck, neither York nor Garret hadn't paid her any mind when they entered her bedroom. What was an eighteen-year-old doing wearing something like that anyways? Those things were made to torture a man. It took too long to get the damn things off and out of the way. They belonged on the floor. All-natural was perfect. But that piece of fabric hugged her in all the right places. Thank fuck I had that hoodie on underneath my kutte tonight, or else I would have been definitely gouging out my own brothers' eyes for even getting a peek at how she looked.

As she went to pull the front door closed, I said, "Leave it fucking open, babe. You ain't coming back."

And like the little defiant streak that was in her, she pulled the door close, but she didn't lock it. Perhaps it was still the worry for her mother that she wanted to make sure whatever she'd left in the house, that Novalie had made an effort to be nice, even though neither of them would care.

We made our way to my truck. I placed the duffle in the back seat as well as the cardboard box, then I looked over my shoulder and saw York climb into the black van.

Then I opened the door for her and helped her in.

As soon as I rounded the truck, I heard a voice from the side of Novalie's house.

"You getting her out of there?" an older lady asked me.

"Yes, I am." If I had it my way, she'd never step foot in that house again.

"Good. Wasn't right. I called social services many times. But somehow that poor excuse of a mother and that man she was with always got wind of when the worker was going to be coming to the house."

"Well, I've got her now. Ain't nothing happening to her." And I meant that with every fiber of my being.

Then I told my brothers that I'd be at the clubhouse in the morning to sort this shit out. But not before I got her settled.

Once I was in the truck, I had to know.

"Kitten, if social services had been called, how did your mom explain away the lack of furniture and shit in the house?"

While she was looking out the window, she answered, "There's a basement. French brings guys to the house to move the furniture from the basement when the worker is there, and they hang fake pictures on the walls."

"What men?"

"You mean you didn't know?" she asked me incredulously while she was looking at me.

"Know what?" I was starting to get ticked off that she would think that of me.

"The prospects from your club."

I pulled my phone up and called York.

"Yeah, Pres?"

"I want all the prospects gathered in the clubhouse first thing in the morning, all the officers, and nobody else. I want that place cleared the fuck out."

"Cotton, yeah, man, but what's going on?" York had never heard me give an order like that either.

"Did you know that French had the prospects doing work for him?" It's one thing for a brother to have a prospect do work for him, but you fucking shared that god damn shit, not asked them to keep quiet. Novalie told me that she heard French telling them if they breathed a word of what they were doing to anyone, they wouldn't get patched in.

"The fuck? What kind of work?" What did it really say when the President and the Vice President didn't know what was going on inside their club?

"Tell you more tomorrow." I didn't need to tell him to make sure they were all there. York would make it so.

Then I could go as far as to say they would have to deal with Garret. Hell, every single one of them would be there bright and fucking early in the morning.

Inhaling and exhaling, I tried to calm myself down.

"You didn't know. I'm sorry, Kane. I had no right." The look she gave me told me as much.

"Yeah, Kitten, you did. Now, let's get fucking home. Yeah?"

"Yeah," she said with a tilt of a smile. The sound of her voice went straight to my dick.

Fuck, this was going to be rough. I needed to get her out of my system. But I knew that was as stupid as saying the sky wasn't blue.

I was in big fucking trouble.

Chapter 4

'Who knew that dreams would turn into reality?'

Novalie

When Cotton had said he was taking us home, I really thought he was talking about the clubhouse, seeing as we drove on the road that led to the clubhouse. Yet as we drove past the clubhouse, we turned on a different road to the left.

This road was paved as well, and it went on for about half a mile. The road had been woven between trees, and with the windows cracked, she could hear the crickets in the woods. Which meant there was likely a creek or a body of water nearby.

And at the end of the drive, I sat there and gazed at the wonder in front of me.

His house wasn't grand by any means, but it was simple, and to me, it was awesome.

The house was a one-story, with light, multi-colored bricks and a two-car garage.

Off to the left, I was shocked as I saw a weeping willow tree. I loved those trees. They stood strong and they looked elegant.

"You have a weeping willow?" I asked, already in love with his house, and I just knew that the inside was going to be just as awesome.

"Yeah, my grandfather planted it for my grandmother." That was a dream you didn't hear about often.

"That's beautiful." And it really was.

"They had their house built on a different spot on the property. Still unsure what to do with it."

"Is it in good shape?"

"Yeah. I keep a check on it. Fix anything that needs fixing." So, he wasn't just the President of an MC. He was a kick-butt mechanic and a handyman. Shoot me now.

"I'm not trying to be nosy or anything but give it to your firstborn or second-born child. Allow them to start something where they'll have meaning. A lot of times, things are always better when there's a history behind it."

"You're right about that. I'll think on it," he said.

When he pressed a button, his garage door opened and he guided the truck in and to a stop. He had tools along the side of the wall and a few trophies. "What are the trophies for?"

"Football. High School." Yes, I could definitely see that about him as well.

"Oh yeah? Were you any good?" Like I even had to ask.

He looked at me and lifted a brow. "You think?"

I chuckled at him. I loved his smile. Well, whenever he gave out a smile.

As we got out of the truck and emptied my things from the back seat, he took me in through the side door.

It led to a mud room and then into the kitchen. The mud room housed the washer and dryer. What I hadn't expected was for the kitchen to be built almost the same as the one in the clubhouse except for the colors. The cabinets were a slate gray in color. The backsplash was a pretty mosaic tile, and the flooring was all light oak. It was beautiful.

He even had a double Dutch oven and a farm-style sink. His dishwasher and his refrigerator were stainless steel as well as all of the appliances on the counter. And on the island and the countertops was a pretty granite marble color.

The kitchen, living room, and dining room were all in one big open floor plan. When I peered into the dining room, I saw a set of French double doors and a deck with a pool.

"You have a pool?" That was something I had never been able to do. Since June didn't have a pool and I didn't have anyone to really take me to the community pool, it was something I never got to experience.

"Yeah, heated too. I'll open it up in a few weeks." That was something that had been on my bucket list ever since I could remember. And thanks to Cotton, I was going to get to experience that.

It would seem that I owed this man much. Probably more than I would ever be able to repay.

"It's heated. Talk about fancy." And the small smile I had received was priceless. Those were few and far between for him. Though it made him even more gorgeous, and he didn't need any help with that.

As he led me through the house and down a hallway, he told me his room and office were down the other side of the house with his bathroom. There were three bedrooms down this hallway with one bedroom and a bath on the left and two bedrooms with a Jack and Jill style bathroom.

It was the room on the left that he led me to. Inside was a wrought iron bed frame, a white dresser, and two white nightstands.

On top of the bed was a dark red down comforter and one of the best-looking, most comfortable beds I'd ever seen.

The nightstands held two lamps. The bathroom was in much the same color scheme as the kitchen, and I imagined that all of the house was in much the same manner.

"Did you design all this house yourself?"

"Yep. It's what I've always wanted."

"It's beautiful, Kane. Really. And umm . . . thanks for letting me stay here. I'll do my best to carry my own weight."

"Kitten, can you cook?" Thankfully, I had learned to cook all by myself. Had I burnt a lot of it at the beginning? Yes, I did. Is it true that you can burn water? Yes, it is. But I had to learn, or else I wouldn't have been able to eat.

"Yeah, I can."

"Okay, you'll carry your own weight in cooking and helping me keep the house tidy."

"But Kane, that's hardly fair . . ." There was no way that was good enough.

"Kitten, the house is paid for. The utilities are not that high. Just help with food and cooking. I'll be good with that."

"Kane . . ." I started.

"Kitten, babe, let it go, yeah. You're safe here. Time for all of it to change for the better." I didn't know what I'd done for him to be in my corner, but I would be eternally grateful for it.

"Okay, Kane."

"Now settle in. And I mean this, make yourself at home." I didn't have much, but I hoped that I wouldn't cramp his style.

And with that, he turned away and left. I inhaled and exhaled, trying to get myself under control and out of being freaked out.

The first thing I did was take a shower. A hot shower. Yes, since I was able to pay the electricity bill, I was able to have hot water, but to be honest, it was always luke-warm at best. The shower at my mom's had nothing on the shower here at Cotton's. Even the faucet had settings to set the water to come out at whatever speed I wanted it.

And I had yet another first. For the first time in my life, I slept like the dead and I didn't even have to lock the bedroom door.

The very next morning when I woke up, I laid there shocked as I looked at the time on my phone. I couldn't remember a time when I'd slept past eight o'clock in the morning, and it was closing in on ten in the morning. Since I just had to log on for my exam score, I didn't have school. Graduation was on Saturday and then I would be out of high school.

When I rolled out of bed in the t-shirt and shorts I slept in, I made my way to the bathroom. I washed my face, brushed my teeth, and finished my business.

Unfortunately, I broke my rule of never going to bed with wet hair. My raven black hair was in a tangled mass of curls, so instead of trying to get my mop of hair into order, I grabbed the hair tie on my wrist and pulled my hair up into a messy bun.

When I looked down at my shirt, I saw it was one of the Wrath MC t-shirts they had been selling at the carnival the town had once a year. The money that was raised went to St. Jude's. It was one of the worthiest causes ever.

That was part of why I wanted to be a NICU nurse. I would love to work at St. Jude's. Even if I didn't get paid, just knowing that I would be there to help those kids who are God's creations get through another day, that would make my world.

After I was done getting ready for the day, I made my way down the hall and to the kitchen. On the big island there was a note,

'Kitten, Headed to the clubhouse. Keys on the counter to the truck. I called

> *Virginia, she said to take a couple days off. Oh, and the pool is open. Go enjoy it. - Kane.'*

That man.

He had to have seen my face when I had gotten a look at the pool.

Well, I never told him that I didn't have my license. Mom was never around to sign the paper for me to even take the drivers ed class. Hopefully, Cotton would be able to help me do that. So, I went to my room and grabbed my phone. As I made my way back to the kitchen, I texted him.

> *Novalie – Mom never signed the paper for drivers ed. I don't have a license.*

A few minutes later, as I was making myself a sandwich, my phone chimed.

> *Kane – Fucking figures. I'll get you a book and take you to get your license next week.*

> *Novalie – K. Thanks.*

While I was eating my sandwich, I took in the contents of his fridge and pantry. I was surprised at how well it was stocked for a bachelor living alone.

Novalie – Are you going to be home for dinner?

I saw pork chops, grabbed them and the ingredients to marinate them.

Kane – Yeah. Need me to get anything?

Novalie – No. Your kitchen is stocked.

After I finished my sandwich, I whipped up the marinade for the pork chops. It was then that I noticed he had potatoes, so homemade mashed potatoes and green beans. I also saw he had some apples, and I would kill for a homemade apple pie.

And I was in luck. I opened the music app on my phone that June had shown me to use and started my playlist.

So that being said I sat everything on the counter to get ready to be made.

But first I had a bucket list to check off. For some reason, Cotton had opened the pool while I was asleep. I didn't know anything about them, but I was very thankful that he had done that for me.

The first time my toe touched the water I froze. Was it supposed to be this freaking cold?

So, I pulled out my phone and texted June. I wished that I knew what was going on with her. We hadn't really texted much since I had gotten my new phone either.

Novalie – Is a pool supposed to be freezing?'

However, it seemed that June had had no intent on replying soon. So, I sat my phone to the side and said to heck with it. The moment I submerged up to my neck, I was freezing. I had taken off my shirt and shorts. The sports bra and the tight underwear wasn't a bikini, but it was the best thing I had.

But then something cool happened, the water heated up. I remembered Cotton telling me that it was heated. And when I walked through the water to a panel on the side of the pool, I could see the degrees going up. I guessed the warmth was set on a timer. *Fancy,* I thought to myself, even for a big bad biker like Cotton.

Before I knew it, I had already been in the pool enjoying myself for two hours. I had looked on YouTube and found a way to stay afloat in the deeper end. And then, when I emerged from the water, I didn't feel the burn.

It hadn't been until I wrapped myself in a towel, went to my shower, and washed off the chlorine before I stepped in front of the mirror while I was drying off. My shoulders were already a light pink.

Thankfully, from being outside a good bit, I knew that I would burn but the next day I'd be tanned. I just had to deal with the light burn for a day.

I started my music playing with my damp hair hanging in loose curls down my back.

As Janis Joplin started with her crooning, I began to peel the apples.

In no time, I was dancing around in his kitchen as my playlist shifted from rock to country to pop and then back to rock with a little R and B mixed in there. I popped the apple pie into the oven, and after I cleaned up my mess, I had a candle and a few others that I wanted to decorate the house with. While I was doing that, I also noticed that June had yet to reply back to my text. It only showed delivered.

After I set the last candle on the mantle, my phone chimed again, only it wasn't the sound of a text but an email. And when I opened the app, there in my inbox, were my scores for the SAT that I took the previous morning.

My first thought was that there had to be something wrong, or I really needed glasses.

My second thought, well, I hadn't realized that I had done it until his voice came through the speaker.

"Yeah, Kitten?" Luckily, I had gotten over the fear of asking him for anything or sharing anything with him.

"Kane . . . I got fifteen hundred and seventy-nine points on my SAT!" I yelled and squealed.

The raucous laughter that came through my speaker meant that Cotton had me on speaker. Whoops.

"Am I on speaker?" I asked even though I knew the answer. I bit my bottom lip, cue the nervousness.

"Yeah, Novalie. I hope that's a good number, darlin'." That was York.

"Yes, that's good. The highest number you can get is sixteen hundred."

"That's awesome, Kitten. So that means what?" I could even hear the slight smile in his voice.

"That means that when I send off my college applications, that number is going to hopefully open the door to some of the best colleges in the country."

It was then that the laughter died down, not in the sense that everyone had stopped talking, but in the sense that the phone had been carried away to somewhere else with less noise.

"Kane?" Did he hang up on me?

"I'm here. Send those applications off, but I want you to get to a place where you're happy before you make your final decision. Can you do that for me?" I silently wondered why he'd asked that of me and why his tone sounded a little off.

"Yes, Kane, I can do that." That was one promise I knew I could keep.

"Okay. Congrats again, Kitten."

"Thanks, Kane." It was the tempo in my voice that dropped to an all-time low whenever I told him thank you for anything.

"Oh, I had a talk with French. He doesn't show up for your graduation ceremony, he's out, so is your mom. Even though the club already voted. But for you, I am giving them one last chance. You cool with that?"

"Yeah, Kane." I had wondered how long French was going to get by with doing the crap he'd been doing.

"Okay, I'll see you when I get home, yeah?"

"Yeah, Kane. Be careful." Hopefully, he would be okay with the little improvements I had made as well.

"Yeah." And with that, we hung up.

I didn't like that he sounded like he didn't like it when I commented about the colleges. Then when he stated that he wanted me to just make sure I was happy before I made my decision.

That I could do, my happiness should always be one of the most important things, and it should come above all others. It was my life to live, after all. It took me time to come to that conclusion, but I did it.

Just like it hadn't been forty-five minutes, the timer for the pie went off. As I took it out of the oven, the smells assaulted me and I couldn't wait to cut into it later on tonight.

I looked at the clock on the stove and saw it was now only one thirty, so I did something that I only did at school or at June's house on occasion.

I turned the television on and flipped through the channels. I settled on TLC, and before I knew it, it was already five o'clock. I jumped up and ran to the kitchen to get started on the rest of dinner.

It was as I put the pork chops in the oven that I heard not one but two Harleys. One of them was pulling into the driveway and the other was pulling out. As I looked out the kitchen window, the one retreating from the house wore the same kutte as Cotton and he threw his hand up.

So, I had a guardian? Of course, it would be Cotton who'd give out that order.

I turned from the window and began peeling the potatoes and started the green beans.

"Smells good in here. Is that apples?" I jumped at the sound of his voice. How could a man as big as he was move around so quietly? Almost like he was part mouse.

As I looked up from the potatoes, I smiled at him. I noticed that he didn't have his kutte on when he entered the kitchen.

"Apple pie. Made from scratch," I said proudly.

He looked impressed. "What else?"

"Pork chops, mashed potatoes, and green beans. Sound good?" I hoped that he enjoyed the meal. It was the first meal I was cooking for Cotton, as well as cooking for anyone other than myself.

"Yeah, Kitten. I'm going to go take a shower."

"Okay. I'm sorry it isn't ready yet. I got caught up watching a show."

"Kitten, don't care. It'll be ready when you have it ready. Yeah?"

"How can you be so calm and chill and still be the President of one of the biggest motorcycle clubs on the east coast?"

"Kitten, I don't know, That's just me." And with that, he turned away. "Oh, and by the way, the little touches you've made, they look good. Just do me a favor and limit the pink, okay?" After he received a nod from me, he went to his bedroom.

Luckily, since he had a state-of-the-art stovetop, it didn't take long for the food to cook and be done.

After I had the plates dished up, Cotton emerged from the hallway.

And then my mouth watered. Did he have to look like a *GQ* magazine cover? He was shirtless and in sweats, with his long honey brown hair damp. His tattoos were on full display.

This was the first time I'd ever seen the tattoos, and I did a mental check, making sure that my jaw wasn't hanging open.

"Where do you usually eat meals at?" I didn't want to inconvenience him with anything. Not after everything that he'd done for me.

"You're going to laugh. But this is the first time that kitchen has really been used." *Please, don't let me have messed up*, I thought to myself.

"I didn't do anything wrong, did I?"

"No, Kitten. This is perfect. If you want to watch some more of that show, we can eat in the living room."

"Yeah, that would be great." That show had really caught my eye and I found that I really liked the thought of doing something as simple as watching TV. It just so happened that it was going to be with Cotton that made it all the more sweeter.

As we settled in, I sat on one end of the couch that faced the television and Cotton sat in the recliner closest to the end of the couch.

"This is great, Kitten," he murmured around a forkful of food.

I smiled at him. "Thanks"

"So, what else with school is there? I figure you're about done," he asked me after he swallowed a bite of mashed potatoes.

I swallowed a piece of pork chop. "I have graduation the day after tomorrow. I told Mom, she said she would be there to take me and pick me up, but I highly doubt it."

"I've got you covered," he said with a wave of his fork.

"Kane, I can't ask you to do that. I'll take a taxi or ride the bus." But that was the wrong thing to say.

Especially then, because he exploded. "Kitten, now, I know you're getting used to all of this and that this is all different for you, but I don't want you refusing my help any longer. You don't tell me about something that you need help with or that you need taken somewhere and you'll see another side of me that you won't like." He stared me down until I caved.

"Okay. Thank you. I have to be there at ten and it's supposed to end at one. Can you get free on Saturday?"

He sighed. "Kitten, I'll be there. Nothing will keep me from it. Yeah?"

"Yeah."

"Oh, I put the driver's ed book on the washing machine. Look that over and I'll take you driving after your graduation."

"Cool. Thanks. I know this is probably out of your zone and all, but is there any way that you could give me a ride to the superstore? Since I don't have to pay for electricity and things, I've got spare money for clothes that I really need."

"Yeah. I gotta swing by the clubhouse and then we can go."

"Oh, do you have a computer in your office that I can use? I'm going to send out a few college applications and then do as you asked."

"Yeah, Kitten. Password is eight, one, two, four."

So, when we finished eating, Cotton cleaned up, saying, "You cooked, I'll clean." He hadn't turned around to see that my jaw was about to kiss the floor.

And then to my delight, he brought me a slice of apple pie as he sat with me and watched *Say Yes To The Dress*, me laughing at some of their choices and Cotton complaining about the costs.

I didn't see spending that kind of money on a wedding dress that I was just going to wear one day, but if it was for the right man, then heck yes, I would wear it and own it.

"Don't forget, I'm taking you to graduation. That's a promise," he told me before we parted ways that night and went to bed.

Again, his actions showed not only me but the world.

The next day, Cotton drove us to the clubhouse on the back of his bike and surprised me when he had told me to bring a book bag to put my purchases in because we're taking the bike and there was only so much that his saddlebags could hold.

He had disappeared as soon as we pulled into the front courtyard. So, I took myself into the clubhouse and settled in with a book that I'd splurged on last night about an alpha man who didn't even hold a candle to Cotton.

To my utter surprise, guess who walked over to me while I had been sitting on one of the couches . . .

Justin.

He apologized for all the crap that he'd done. I didn't trust that boy as far as I could throw him, and that said a lot since he had about sixty pounds on me.

Chapter 5

'Knock Knock Motherfucker.'

Cotton

I was still reeling from the events that had taken place on Wednesday when I had picked Novalie up at her house, saving her from that asshole trying to break into her house and do god knows what to her. The tape, the rope, and the condoms that Knox had pulled from the truck.

It was two days later, and I was still wound up from that night. I hadn't slept a wink, with thoughts of what the contents in the man's bag had meant for my Kitten.

It was my fault for not laying down the law more with my brothers and that started on the night when Novalie had told me she hadn't celebrated her birthday since she was twelve, and that had only been when a friend of hers had given her a cupcake at school.

One small measly cupcake.

To be honest, I hadn't ever felt the need to really lay the law down. Most of the time, my brothers were the best of the best, but apparently, it seemed they had that one bad apple and sadly, it only hindered the club as a whole.

Normally, I would let Garret handle anything that concerned the club in that way. But this was on me, so I had further laid down the law with French and booted his ass right the hell out. It was one thing to not pay attention to her even though she is his stepdaughter, but when a young woman gets woken up to someone inside her house while her parents, who had sworn to protect her above all others, had been gone. I'd be damned if I ever found a woman who I wanted to be the mother of my children and make them feel any less important than my whole world.

So, that morning after, when I had driven to the clubhouse, I wasn't exactly abiding by the speed limit.

I'd been in a perpetual bad mood since I had closed my bedroom door the night prior. And my first smile that morning had been from the son of a bitch screaming like the little pansy assed fuck that Frankie was known to be.

Frankie was, for all intents and purposes, the go-to man, and the cheapest man to get ahold of. He would do anything for any amount of money, which would in turn go to blow that he would either snort up his nose or inject into his favorite vein.

Those screams that were coming from the shed also meant that Garret was in there with him. He only knew two other people who could entice those kinds of screams from someone.

One was my brother, Knox. The next was me, and lastly, you had Garret.

From those screams, Garret was having a good damn morning.

But because we had to deal with this bullshit, I placed a call and called in a marker. Powers was near the area where Dale had told him French's cell was pinging. I wanted the pleasure of busting his head in. Unfortunately, I had gotten the call a few minutes ago that French and Amy were nowhere to be found.

Either they were way better than we were giving them credit for, or they had to have an inside source. That information was going to come to light whether the two of them liked it or not.

When I entered the dimly lit room, the usual smells assaulted me. The piss, the vomit, the smell of fresh copper. Plus, the smell of fear. You've never meted out justice unless you knew that smell like it was your aftershave.

"Tell me what I want to know. If not, I'll finish breaking every bone in your hand. Bet your dick is going to miss that hand," Garret drawled out.

"He give you anything?" I asked, seeing the detrimental amount of deformation that was already present on his face and in his hand.

You could see his hand was swollen up and a few bones were poking out of his skin.

"Yeah, but you ain't going to like it. Hell, I'm still having an issue understanding it." And that was huge for the six-foot-five, built like a brick shithouse to say.

"Tell me." I didn't like where this conversation was headed.

"The person who hired him, paid him twenty-three thousand in cash. It was a woman. Fucker won't give me the name, but I can only think of one person who would want to harm Novalie."

"Fucking bitch." I pulled out my phone and called Dale.

I doubted he would be awake seeing as he was never up before noon. So, instead, I popped off a text that I wanted Amy found and I wanted her found now.

"Frankie, you know me. You know my reputation. There's more, isn't there?" I was tired of the back and forth with them seeming to be one step ahead at all times.

"Look. Fuck. Rumor is that the bitch who hired me and her man are hooked up with an MC. Not yours,"

Frankie rushed out to say, as if it was going to save his life or some shit.

"And you couldn't fucking tell me that three god damn hours ago?" Garret yelled in his face. "Don't y'all get that the quickest way to have all of this shit taken care of and out of the way is to tell the fucking truth? Hell, maybe it'll save your life, telling the truth from the beginning. I highly doubt it, but it's there."

As always, Garret gave the truth. That man could spot a lie from fifty yards away. One lie to that man and you were done for. It was no wonder he hadn't settled down and found a mother for his daughter.

The only woman who I'd found in my thirty-five years of life who hadn't lied not once to me was Novalie. My Kitten.

I had an inkling that Dale's information had been correct, only I didn't really want to hear that.

"You're not the one I'm scared of," Frankie said through clenched teeth as he looked at Garret when he put pressure on the already broken fingers.

"Motherfucker, I just broke the whole right side of your hand," Garret growled out.

"Yeah, and that can be fixed, but having my dick sawed off and then set on fire, that can't be fucking fixed. I've seen Cotton do that with my own eyes."

Yeah, and Frankie fucked up his whole damn life when he laid his damn hands on my Kitten.

"Man's got a point," I said as I looked at Garret.

"At least it was the smartest thing you've done so far, Frankie." Then I gave the nod to Garret and walked out of the shed with Frankie screaming for me to come back.

So, I waited on one of the picnic tables for Garret to exit, and when the screams finally stopped, Garret came out and two of the prospects went in for cleanup duty.

"Is it done?" Like I even had to ask.

"Yeah, Pres," he told me while he wiped his hands on a rag that would be doused in bleach and then set to flame.

"Alright, have Knox do his thing if he's in the mood. Then have Walker help him take Frankie for a long vacation."

"You got it." Only before Garret could get in touch with Knox, there he was.

"Wasn't eavesdropping, Pres. I've got it," Knox said as he exited the shed to the farthest right, where he went whenever he had to terrorize someone.

Garret was the club's Enforcer, and he was damn good at his job. I didn't think that Garret's level of madness could ever be topped, but Knox was a close second.

Furthermore, I didn't see how Garret handled his daughter with delicate care. If I hadn't seen it with my own eyes then I would swear that whoever told me that, they didn't know Garret.

With all of that, I headed home and was shocked as fucking all get out the moment that I had walked in through the door.

The smells that wafted from my kitchen had been to die for. Then the little candles that I saw she'd lit not only made it feel more welcoming in my home, but I didn't really think that it was due to the candles. No, it was because Novalie was there.

And the sight of her standing in my kitchen shaking that delectable ass to one of her songs . . . fuck me.

But the moment she had kissed my cheek before she had turned in that night, that had made the day easier to wash off.

That night, I had tasted the most delicious pie I'd ever put in my mouth. It was all buttery and flaky with just the right amount of spice.

I cleaned up our meal and when I settled in for the night to watch some show that seemed to have enraptured her, I wouldn't have minded to spend every night exactly like that. However, I had to keep other thoughts that fought to burst forth at bay.

It had still sickened me at the meager belongings that she did have. So, after we had gotten up and headed to the clubhouse, I ventured off to handle a few things and take care of a matter in the motorcycle bay.

With all of that done, I strode into the clubhouse to find my Kitten curled up on the couch with her nose buried in a book on her phone. How did I know that? From the amount of concentration she was giving the screen.

It was when I offered her my hand to help her up that she seemingly snuggled herself further into my being when she tisked at me.

"Kane, let's go take care of that hand." In the motorcycle bay, I had busted my knuckles more than a few times trying to get a motor back on a bike.

"Kitten, my hand's fine." It wasn't the first time and it damn sure wouldn't be the last.

"Yeah, and it will be after I disinfect those cuts."

The look I gave her should have sent shivers down her spine.

"Kane, really? Let's go, you stubborn ass," she muttered.

Grumbling with my tail tucked between my legs, I followed her with my hand placed firmly into her much smaller one.

Once she disinfected my cuts and applied some kind of ointment on them, she deemed my hand would be good.

Something I would never tell a soul, that other than a nurse and a doctor, Novalie taking care of me was the first time that anyone had ever cared for me since my mom passed away when I was five.

We mounted the bike, and I took her to the local superstore. The store held everything. I laughed when he saw her nose turn up at some of the uppity selections that the store carried. When she had laid eyes on clothes that were more her style, I laughed even more.

It took all of my persuasion to finally get her to agree to get whatever her heart desired because I was paying for it. For thirty minutes we had that conversation while people kept walking by no doubt laughing at the slip of a thing that was throwing sass at a big biker.

"Thank you, Kane," she said so low that I almost missed it. After we had to buy another bag to put her purchases in, we somehow managed to strap it to the back of the bike.

That night, I laid in bed, smiling fucking wide for the first time in my life. However, that night, I also got up out of bed and went to her room. With her door cracked open, I walked in and for a good fifteen minutes, I stood there like a maniac, watching the rise and fall of her chest with her breathing, just needing to make sure that she was real.

Friday had come and gone in a blur and then it was time to get ready for her graduation ceremony.

French and Amy were supposed to be back for her graduation ceremony, and I hoped like hell they were there, for Novalie's sake.

But like normal, they failed Novalie again, time after time after time.

If it hadn't been for her telling me about the ceremony when I hadn't stopped prying about events and things where she needed someone to be there, I figured she would've endured the big moment alone.

I had already decided I was going to be there for her. She was just going to have to get used to all the ways that I intended.

That morning came and neither French nor Amy would answer their phones, and it again went straight to voicemail. However, I gave them one more chance to get their shit and get out of town and not be gunned down.

So, while Novalie was getting ready, I donned a black button-up shirt and a certain color tie with crisp new jeans and my kutte. I would be damned if my Kitten didn't have someone there on an important day.

Except other jackasses were trying to ruin that plan.

"Hey, Kane, York is here," Novalie said from outside my bedroom.

"Yeah. Send him in, Kitten." All York had to do was pick up the phone.

It was in that instance that York stuck his head in.

"Pres, we got a problem. I thought this deserved a face-to-face," York said.

"What now?" I sighed. Could we not go a damn day where shit wasn't hitting the fan every second?

"Spades MC is saying we hijacked their shipment." York looked like he didn't even believe it himself.

"They've been smoking that good shit or something? We don't hijack a damn thing. We don't need to. Think they're aware that we know French was giving them cash?"

"I know that. I don't know, Pres, but I do want to know what is really going on. What do you want me to tell them?"

"I've got somewhere I have to be. Schedule a meet first thing in the morning. I'll not start this off with putting her on the back burner like everyone else has done to her."

"Who?" York asked.

"Novalie."

"Ah. You need any company? It ain't right what they've been doing to her." Hell, my brothers didn't even know the half of it. I doubted they ever would.

"Yeah, see if any of the brothers want to go, but leave a few bodies at the clubhouse. Her fucking mom still hasn't shown up. We leave in thirty minutes." If any of his brothers wanted to come with us, it would also be a show to Novalie that they had her back just as well as I did. And that was important. I would forever be kicking my own ass for letting her down all these years.

"Ten-four," I heard York say as he pressed the phone to his ear and told Sanchez as he was walking out the door that they would have the sit-down tomorrow.

Long as nobody was dying or having a baby, I was going to her graduation.

When Novalie had told me all that shit that had been going on, it had torn my heart right out of my chest.

A crimson-colored tie hung around my neck and I was ready.

And it was well worth it as soon as I saw her exit from her bedroom as she saw the color of my tie.

Since she did her hair, it fell in long ringlets down her back, I decided that we were taking my truck.

No way was she getting messed up on the back of my bike.

"You look beautiful, Kitten. Are you ready?"

"Nice tie. Ready as I'll ever be." I fucking hated the resigned expression that marred her beautiful face. Fucking. Hated. It.

"She still hasn't called, has she?" She knew who I was asking about.

"No. And sadly, it doesn't surprise me."

To my surprise, she didn't like the fact that we were taking the truck, and she made it known. So, in a fashion that was her, she hiked her dress up that she had shorts on underneath and pulled back her hair, then when she was ready, she climbed on the back of my bike.

Like a loon I was vastly becoming whenever I was with her, I was smiling the whole way to my bike.

It was as we were pulling out of the driveway that we were surrounded by my brothers. The fifteen of them followed us to the citizen center, and even Cree was on the back of Garret's bike, with Lucy on the back of Dale's.

As we pulled up front and parked our bikes, my Kitten received a lot of looks, and I noticed most of them were shock and awe, but there had been a few condescending ones as well. Those could eat shit.

As my Kitten stepped up on the stage in her white gown and gold graduation cap, I hollered loudly, as did all of my brothers in the MC. Did we get all heads turned in our direction? Yep. Did we give a shit? Hell no.

She was smiling at her teachers and then as she stepped off the stage, I figured she would go sit with her class like all the others were doing, but that's not what she did.

Like the little rebel she was, she continued walking past where they were pointing her to go and came walking up to me.

"Thanks for coming, Kane. All of you. This means so much to me." I saw the tears forming in her blue eyes, but those were tears of happiness.

"Told you I wouldn't let you down, Kitten."

"I know." Then spectators be damned, she hurled herself at me and I threw my head back and laughed as I caught her. When I brought my head back down, I kissed her forehead.

She was officially an adult. She was going for her driver's license next week.

After the ceremony had ended and pictures were taken, I gave her lessons in my truck and she aced them in a split second. That was a good thing, considering I had planned on giving her my truck to drive.

That night, we had a party at the clubhouse that had only been for Novalie.

And two people who should have been there hadn't even bothered, which everyone noticed.

It had been decided at church that they had to have gone underground but we just didn't know where. Yet.

***

A few weeks had passed and, yes, she did get her license with the same megawatt smile on her face when she came to me with her license in her hands. And I smiled wide when I saw that it was my address on her license and not her parents'.

We had come to be on a schedule. When we woke up, she made breakfast and I pulled out after her to head to the clubhouse as she pulled out and went to work at the diner. She kept to her promise. She'd received acceptance letters to a lot of colleges. There had even been some she hadn't applied to, but they were asking her to apply.

It wasn't until a couple days after Fourth of July, and on my birthday, when I realized that I'd made a big mistake.

I had been with the MC that whole day on the bike, and I'd left my Bluetooth headphones at the house, so I had missed a few calls from her after six.

When I had gotten home, I saw that apparently, she'd made a quiet celebration dinner for my birthday. I had told her I would be there around six, and I knew she had texted asking me when I would be there after it had passed six, but I hadn't ever replied to her.

I had been about to earlier, but then something was said and texting her back had slipped my mind. Hence the phone calls that I hadn't been able to hear as well.

Unfortunately, I didn't get home until eleven that night. She was a vision in an off-the-shoulder shirt and leggings, her hair all flayed out on the edge of the couch, where she had fallen asleep.

As I took in the house, I glanced at the kitchen table and saw two candles that were burned halfway down. There was a dish of meat loaf, my favorite, a bowl of mashed potatoes, a bowl with gravy, corn on the cob, and rolls.

Then that was when I smelled it—a fucking peach cobbler.

First, I was going to put her to bed, and second, I was going to see what I could do to salvage the food so we could eat this meal tomorrow.

As I bent down to pick her up in my arms, it had to be the jostle that awoke her.

She was sleepy and even then, half-asleep, hearing my name on her lips . . . fuck. "Kane?" It had done something to me, and it further proved that shit had changed.

"It's me, babe. Sorry I'm late." I rarely apologized, but to her I seemed to do it a lot.

"It's okay. Everyone, okay?" she murmured, almost as if she were falling back asleep.

"Yeah, Kitten, just club business." She was always worried and checking in on the men, even though they had all, myself included, treated her like trash. That wasn't okay then and it wasn't okay now.

"Okay." And then a light snore assaulted my ears. It was the cutest thing I'd ever heard in my life.

When I went to her bedroom, I turned down her covers with one hand, laid her down, and kissed her forehead. It was then that I saw the picture.

It was Novalie and me at the clubhouse, right after the July Fourth celebration we held every year. We had just gotten on the bike when Cree came over to us and said, "Say cheese."

I had on my shades and hadn't put on my helmet yet, so my hair had been tied back. Novalie's hair was in a side braid that she was known for. She had on her shades as well. She still had her hands on my shoulders because she had just climbed on. And there in the picture was my Kitten with a megawatt smile on her face and I even had a lift at the corner of my mouth.

    I made a mental note to get with Cree and get that picture. I wanted it hung up on the wall in the living room. And I would make it a point to see what other pictures Cree had of my Kitten.

Chapter 6

'When push comes to shove,

knock the heifer out.'

Novalie

It had been a few days after we had re-celebrated Cotton's birthday when the club was having their No Holds Barred Beat Down. Members came from all their other chapters that they had started up recently with Cotton being the first founding member. And they even had other clubs that were allies there too to compete tonight.

They drew numbers to see who had to fight who, and the winner got to challenge Cotton. Should a man ever beat him, then he would have first chance at unseating his presidency.

And still to this day eighteen years later no one had bested him. However, that night, only one of the men had come close and that man was Garret.

Unfortunately for the other men, Cotton had some hidden moves that nobody really knew about until that afternoon. Beers and shots had been passed around when Cotton had been named the victor. And as all of his MC gathered around him, he called for me.

So, I grabbed him a cold beer and brought it over to him. The moment I had been in arm's reach, he hauled me to him and kissed my forehead. These past few weeks had been a dream for me, and that dream was a great reality.

"Let's hear it for the old man!" York called out.

"You damn motherfucker," Cotton chuckled out.

York laughed, "Well, it's true." I could see the wheels churning in Cotton's mind from my place under his arm.

"You're the fucking one with gray in your hair already, you fucker." Well, that I didn't know. I thought York was actually quite a few years older than Cotton because of that fact.

I had my answer when York obviously saw the confusion on my face, and he told me that he was twenty-seven and the early gray hair was hereditary.

Standing in line at the buffet tables, I was watching Cotton with some of the kids in the MC on the playground that they'd built a couple weeks ago. It was a stark contrast to the man that everyone knew.

I stood there laughing to myself that Cotton had gotten me back tenfold a few days ago. I had made him some tea. Only I supposedly forgot to add the sugar and the moment he spit the shit out all over the island, I'd roared with laughter. So hard in fact that I'd had tears coming out of my eyes.

It had been the day after our Fourth of July celebration, he'd placed 'pop its' underneath the toilet seat in my bathroom. Imagine my shock and surprise at hearing a bunch of cracks and blue lights flashing beneath my bare bottom at five after one in the morning, when I was still half asleep and feeling like a zombie.

Oh, but I definitely got my payback. To my delight, however, when he emerged from the shower, still wet and in a towel, he had vanilla yogurt in his long hair and beard. But it was when I turned to laugh my ass off silently that he'd gotten his revenge.

Apparently, he didn't like it so much that I had put vanilla yogurt into his shampoo bottle. The fallout from that resulted in me being grabbed from behind and being thrown into the pool in the backyard when we had about eight of the MC members there to grill out.

The pool, mind you, had just opened a month ago and it was early in the morning, so was the water warm? That was a big fat freaking negative. And that was because the timer for the heater wasn't set to come on because of the summertime. I had come up yelling and sputtering for all I was worth. I don't curse so I had to be very animated with the words I'd thrown at him.

"Not too bad for an old man." I knew the moment those words came from my mouth; I'd made a big mistake.

Especially when I heard the mumbled words under his breath as he'd turned from the pool and headed back inside the house. "I'll fucking show you old."

I wasn't sure what he'd meant with that statement. And then a shiver swept through my body, no it hadn't been from the pool water because the water was slightly warm. No, it was from Cotton possibly showing more of himself, which meant more to me than I even wanted to admit.

Our lines of friendship were vastly being breached and then thrown back over that line like a bucket of cold water.

I knew that if I wanted that man, and want him I definitely did, then I needed to desperately make my feelings for him known. But first, sadly, I had to get through a date tomorrow with a boy.

That boy who'd been hounding me at the diner. Every single time he came in, he asked me out. It was like clockwork. So, when I realized he wasn't going to stop, I told him I would go out on one date with him if he would stop asking me.

Something I also told myself would be good for me, especially if I could find someone else to take my feelings away from Cotton, if he didn't feel the same.

Returning back to the present I moved along with the line of people at the buffet-style tables, making their plates.

After I had my plate and one for Cotton full, even with macaroni salad, which he hated, I made my way over to him.

And the sight that I saw made my blood boil. Cotton wasn't mine, my brain knew that, but my heart, no it chose Cotton. No matter what happens he will always be the man that I compare every other member of the male population to.

"Vas." I smiled at her.

Vas was one of the club girls, she was standing a little too close to Cotton for my liking. No, I didn't have a claim on him, but I wouldn't stand there beside him like he liked while some woman was rubbing herself all over him.

"Novalie." The way Vas said my name had me cringing. She said it through her nose. No, it wasn't really the way that Vas talked, but it was in the way that she had come across. Almost as if she was trying to stake her claim.

I repeated to myself, *honey sweetness everything.*

"Can you move over to the side a bit?" I needed to hand Cotton his plate, but I really wanted Vas to move away. See I had been nice.

"Now, why would I do that?" Vas had a smug expression on her face as she tried to glide closer to Cotton. Funny thing was, Cotton stepped further off to the side.

"Because I'm about five seconds from making you move myself. And I'd rather have you as a friend than an enemy, especially since us women are few and far between. Not to mention, Cotton keeps stepping away from you, he doesn't like to feel caged in." If this girl didn't heed my warning? Well, I wasn't so inclined to fight anyone, but at this very moment, if that didn't work, then I wouldn't hesitate.

Then a look that Vas was surprised became evident across her face. "You want me as a friend?"

"Well, yeah, why wouldn't I?" I didn't have any beef with anyone in the club. Besides, I didn't want to. Not when I had learned from an early age that it was rare to find someone that you could call a true friend.

A few breaths passed, then Vas stepped to the side. It didn't escape my notice, or anyone else's for that matter, that Vas then moved closer to Garret, the club's stoic and unmovable Enforcer, unless your name was Cree.

"Thanks, Vas. I'm going to the mall tomorrow to hit up Body Works, they're having a huge mega-sale. Want to go with me?" I asked her as I handed Cotton his plate.

"I think I would like that," The look that came across Vas's face said it all as I offered her that line of friendship.

"Mind if I tag along? I need some new scents and such," Lucy asked from underneath Dale's arm.

"Yeah, totally. We can make a day of it. I'd invite Cree, but she has practice in the morning," I told the women.

"Awesome." Yeah, Lucy was cool. She was basically the club mom of us all. She was the first original ole' lady.

"Kitten, why the fuck did you put this fucking mac salad on my plate?" There it was his response to his plate.

"Because you said you had to watch your figure, Kane. I was just helping you out." I tried to appear all innocent, and when he took a bite of the salad, his facial expression was hilarious.

The group around us chuckled.

"Shut it," Cotton grumbled. And they all listened, except me of course, because I was still laughing with each cringe he made as he chewed and swallowed.

"Kitten, you're pushing it," he stated in his serious tone that seemingly never affected me.

"Yeah, yeah, I've heard that before. Oh, can you lend me, Lucy, and Vas one of the prospects tomorrow? A store in the mall is having a mega sale." I knew he hadn't been listening to us as we had made our plans.

"Yeah. I'll have Xavier go with y'all." Then he did what he normally did whenever he agreed to my little requests—he dipped his head and kissed the top of my head.

And just like that, everyone was staring at us. I could see the shocked expressions on their faces.

Heck, I was still shocked at some of the little things that he had been doing lately. The little touches, the texts, the making sure he had eyes on me when I was in another room than him at the clubhouse.

However the spell between us had been broken, "You coming to the clubhouse with me Friday night?" he asked as he took another bite of the salad wincing as he did so.

We were having a poker night, something that was new.

I bit my bottom lip, sadly, I really didn't want to tell him. Had Cal backed off, I wouldn't be in this position, freaking men. "Actually, I have plans for Friday night."

Cotton looked at me with a raised brow. "Plans," he growled.

"Well a… date… actually," it took everything in me not to look away from his gaze that seemed to be getting angrier by the second.

"A date," his tone was low.

I didn't know how to defuse the situation, Cotton was glaring at me, however, Garret seemed to know that Cotton was about to blow his top when he asked, "You talk to your mom, Novalie?"

I knew Cotton had shared a lot of what was going on with my mom and French.

"No. I tried to call her when I thought I needed her signature for a form for my license, but Cotton told me that since I was eighteen, they wouldn't require her signature."

"Gotcha. Look, something I need to ask you. You're pretty close with my girl, and she's going through something and won't talk to me. Any way you can talk to her?"

"Can I speak to you in private right quick?" This wasn't something that other ears needed to be listening to.

With an eyebrow raised, he said, "You can speak freely."

"No offense meant to anyone here, but this isn't a conversation that Cree would want to have heard." I wouldn't betray my friend in that way.

A look of respect crossed Garret's face. "Gotcha."

I followed him a few steps away. It was when we were face to face about ten feet away from everyone that I answered his question.

"The reason why Cree is kind of out of sorts is her studies, because some of her teachers won't take the time to break the material down for her. She can't seem to get ahead and some of the kids at school have been bullying her, but she didn't want you to know. On top of that, her feminine friend has yet to visit her, and a lot of the girls on the softball team have already gotten theirs."

"Fuck, I had no damn idea." A painful expression was now across his face

"To be honest, she needs another woman who she can talk to outside of the club that will be there just for her, I think. Someone separate. Oh, and a tutor. But seriously, you've done great with her. Cree is strong-willed and an amazing person. And she's lucky to have a dad who cares."

"Thanks. I've been meaning to find someone to help her out, but everyone I've found keeps coming on to me." He looked horrified at that too.

"I get that, and I'm sorry. Can I ask you a question?"

"Yeah."

"Just say by some miracle if you would have beaten Cotton, would you have tried to take his presidency?" He knew why I was asking him that.

Garret looked down at me differently then, "Well, seeing as that will never happen, no. Cotton is a good man."

"I know. I would have jumped in the ring to prevent that myself. I could bring you to your knees, buster," I joked jovially.

"I'd like to see you try." he told me as he bumped my shoulder with his.

What I didn't see was the glare that Cotton had been shooting at Garret.

That night, the party raged on, Vas and I had some illegal mixtures in our cups. We had been laughing and carrying on until two men walked over to where we were sitting.

The one to the right offered Vas his hand, and because she was a club girl, she had to get up and dance with a brother from another chapter as was in her duties.

The second guy offered me his hand, but before I could decline, Cotton slid in front of me with his arms crossed as he shook his head.

When the man realized he wasn't going to get what he wanted, he turned and walked away. Then Cotton turned to me. "You ready to go, Kitten?" Maybe he did have the same feelings for me as I did for him. I freaking hoped so.

"Yeah, Kane." I grabbed our cups then walked by Cotton's side, tossed them in the trash can that was set up near the door.

As soon as he parked the bike in the garage, he turned to me, "Now, I want to know why you haven't been smiling like usual when you head to the diner. What's going on?"

So I broke down and told him about what had been going on at the diner. The new manager that Virginia had hired seemed to have it out for me, she didn't step in when the customers got too rowdy with me, she only stepped in with the other waitresses. Not to mention, she had me do all of the cleaning, and I got all of the crappy tables. It was why I hadn't really been looking forward to going into work.

It was at that moment that he told me he would have Xavier come into the diner whenever I was to be on shift. He also told me that he would talk to Virginia and just tell her it was for his peace of mind.

Once we got into the house, we went our separate ways, as soon as my head hit the pillow, I passed out.

What I didn't know was that Cotton stood outside my doorway while he watched me sleeping until the wee hours of the morning.

As soon as I woke up, I dressed, put on some light makeup, then took the truck to the clubhouse. As soon as we all loaded up, we hit the road, with Xavier right behind us.

As soon as we hit the mall, we spent way too much money with Xavier carrying our bags.

Vas had pulled us into a store that Xavier had refused to go in.

"I'm not risking Cotton's wrath if he found out I followed you into this store. I'll wait out here." I looked at Xavier with a raised brow as he smirked, then took up his position at the door.

It was Victoria's Secret and some new lingerie had been purchased by the three of us. I needed to hang out with these ladies more often.

The next afternoon, I was on the couch flipping through channels, I decided now was as good a time as any. Pulling up my big girl panties so to speak, I took a deep breath then said, "Kane, can I ask you something?"

"Yeah." He stopped and wiped his hands on a greasy rag since he had been in the garage, no doubt working on his second bike that he mentioned he wanted to sell a while back.

"Do you remember when you told me you hated telling a lie and you said that you told a lie to me?" Cotton appeared to have been calm and collected, but judging by the change in his body language, he was anything but.

That conversation had taken place that night after he had thrown me in the pool.

After everyone had left we had been sitting around the fire pit in the backyard.

"Tell me something you've never told anyone?"

He had looked at me with a raised brow, I wasn't sure whether he would do it or not, however, when he opened his mouth I was shocked.

"Done a lot of shit in my life Kitten, things that would make a lesser man cower, but there's only one thing I regret, and that's lying to you." Before I could respond and ask him what he had lied to me about, he had stood up and went back into the house.

For the next hour I had been wracking my brain trying to figure out what he could possibly be talking about.

"Kitten, now's not the time, yeah," he said as he turned and walked away from me.

"Then when is the time, Kane?" I called after him, and he stopped, like usual anytime I pushed something. It wasn't often that I pushed but when I did, it was usually something extremely important to me.

"Kitten, you're not going to let this go, are you?" He knew me all too well.

"No. I really want . . . no, I need to know."

"Why?"

Did I really have to open up and tell him? Tell him about the electric shocks that I feel every time our skin connects. Did I tell him that every time I laid eyes on him, I got butterflies?

"Because I need to know if I'm the only one with these feelings," I said as I stared at my legs criss crossed in front of me.

"Kitten," I heard. It was then that I lifted my head and looked into his eyes across the living room.

"Kane, please. I don't ask for much, but this is important." When his body relaxed, I knew I had him. I was about to get my answer. I hoped like heck it was what I wanted to hear.

"Fine. When you asked me how I could be so calm and chill and still be the President of one of the biggest motorcycle clubs on the east coast, and I told you it was just me?"

"Yes, I remember."

"That was when I lied to you. It isn't just me. I'm only like this with one person on this planet."

"Who then?" I could feel myself coming close to tears. It was something I hated. I wasn't a pretty crier, I was one of the ones with snot, red cheeks, and puffy eyes.

"Kitten. You." And there went my guards and my walls, and in he went. Safe and sound, he wrapped himself neatly around my heart.

"Kane, I don't ever see you as a father figure, nor an uncle, and definitely not a guardian. I don't see us as just simply friends either, don't think I ever really did." I bit my bottom lip and waited for an answer. If it was the right answer, I'd be whipping out my phone and cancelling that date.

However, as minutes passed by, he said not one word.

But then he did. "I've got to go get ready. Got plans." Before that, my heart had been so full and near bursting, then just like that, it was splayed wide the heck open, visible and shattered for all to see.

I was not going to have a pity party. I was not going to feel sorry for myself. I told him how I felt, and it was obvious that he didn't feel the same.

So, I went and got ready for my date. A date with a boy who was persistent. His name was Cal, and he was nowhere near as tall as Cotton, but he was at least five-foot-ten.

I donned a nice pair of faded blue jeans and pulled on my new boots that Cotton had bought for me as a graduation present. I'd never been one for accessories but these damn boots, I loved them. The next to go on was a soft pink cashmere sweater. I braided my hair on the top part only and pulled the rest of it up into a ponytail, not that I was trying to get Cotton's attention anymore, but I really liked that he had said he liked my hair like that. Next, I put in some dangly earrings. After I spritzed some perfume on, I put on some light makeup which consisted of eyeliner, mascara, and some lip gloss.

By the time I was ready, it was seven o'clock. My date was apparently going to be a few minutes late.

As I exited my room, I saw Cotton bent over the island with his hands outstretched on either side of him. As if he heard me coming or sensed I was near, he turned his head.

As soon as he gave me a once over, he looked away. I almost missed it. "You look nice, Kitten."

"Thanks." I smiled a sad smile at him. "What about you? You clean up very nice." And he did look nice. He had on nice fitting jeans and a black button-down shirt with his kutte, and his long hair was pulled up in a man bun.

"Kitten, this ain't me cleaning up." If this wasn't what he called himself cleaned up, then I wasn't going to let my imagination get the best of me. But talk about if the man put on a suit. Sweet baby Jesus.

Our conversation was still on repeat in my mind as soon as I had walked out the door with Cal. His whole 'Kitten, this ain't me cleaning up', that had definitely started something heating up inside of me, a feeling I only experienced when I was with Cotton.

I hadn't liked the look on Cotton's face when I had left the house and climbed into Cal's car.

As I had followed Cal into the restaurant, this was one night that I seriously wanted to end so I could get back home, if only to be near Cotton. Even though he didn't return the same feelings, maybe I could work on him. Eventually.

However, being out with Cal, it didn't make me feel anywhere near as safe. We had gone to one of the most established high-end restaurants in our area. I smiled at the hostess and also noticed that Cal didn't know how to keep his eyes in his head.

Cotton, he didn't so much as look at another woman while he was with me. Even when we were at the club and there had been some hot ass women there, and yes, I had no problem admitting it either.

Cal also seemed to be an ass man, judging by all the looks he was giving every single woman who stood up and walked near our table.

Whether Cal saw it or not, the women he was staring at were nothing on the looks that I was getting from every man as I glanced around the restaurant. My skin was continuing to crawl even more so.

And what further ruined my night was when Cal ordered for me and it was a salad. A freaking salad. No, I wasn't a small girl by any means, but I also wasn't overweight.

"It isn't like you need more than a salad." Hadn't he been the one chasing me?

It had taken all I had inside of myself to not whip out my phone and call Cotton. I needed to stand up for myself and not rely on Cotton to fix everything.

However, I was about to throw my napkin onto the table and leave because Cal had just licked his lips at a woman who had walked by our table.

What I didn't notice in my heightening fury was that I didn't need to worry about calling Cotton. Not when a sudden hush had settled over the restaurant, and that hush was caused by a monster of a man wearing a black button-down shirt, jeans, motorcycle boots, and a Wrath MC kutte.

And let's just say that Cotton hadn't missed the fact that the man ordered me a salad, and that Cotton was furious about Cal's comment to me. Just to add salt to the wound, the disrespect he had shown me a second ago definitely didn't add anything helpful.

Then the moment Cotton had opened his mouth as soon as he had reached our table, I wanted to jump from my chair and plant myself as deeply in his arms as I could manage. I would settle for his heart first.

Oh, to the woman who was lucky enough to get this man.

In the next instance, it appeared that I should have had just a tad bit more faith in myself.

Chapter 7

'Nothing like sliding into home.'

Cotton

As I was getting ready, I was really starting to regret my conversation with Ashley a few days ago in the grocery store. Had Novalie not told me she had a date on Friday, I never would have agreed to what I had.

"Hey, Cotton," a woman had said from behind me while I'd been in line buying groceries for the house. I'd been laughing at myself.

Surprisingly, I didn't snarl at the fact that over half the shit that was littering the conveyer belt was girly as fuck. Who the hell drank almond milk, and not to mention the Greek yogurts? Not a man.

On top of that, who in the fuck liked shit in their coffee? Coffee was black, and that was the only way to go.

"Ashley," I stated, trying to be friendly.

"It's good to see you. Looks like you're still watching your figure, huh?" She chuckled. She had asked me a few months back and I'd told her I was dieting and had to watch my figure.

Can you believe the line actually worked, she had just smiled and walked away? Now, it seems she doesn't want to give up.

"Yeah, guess you could say that." *I stood there staring at her body. But fuck if it made me hard at all. Her body didn't compare to Novalie's. But damn if I wasn't getting tired of not being with a woman.*

"Want to go grab a bite to eat Friday night?" *God, I didn't even want to go to eat with her, but I would be damned if Novalie was going out on a date while I sat at home fucking twiddling my damn thumbs.*

"Yeah, that sounds nice. Pick me up at seven?" *Her smile was up to her eyes, like she just won the prize of the year.*

"Yeah, see you then." *And with that, I turned back then finished checking out.*

As soon as I'd gotten home, I'd seen Novalie out back in the pool. I smiled to myself, because the last time she'd been in the pool, I'd tossed her in after she put fucking yogurt in my shampoo.

Normally, Novalie had her bedroom door open. It has been almost two hours now. Something akin to loss was wrapping itself around my neck. Our earlier conversation played on repeat in my mind. She didn't see me as a father figure, a brother figure, or even an uncle. Nor did she see me as a guardian. What she did see in me was maybe more than a friend.

155

I was still kicking my own ass for walking away from our conversation that was way overdue. She turned eighteen at that party over a month ago and I was thirty-six. Luckily, the MC world was very different from the civilians'.

It didn't start out as a robbing the cradle story. What it did was slowly morph into the stories that mothers tell their daughters for bedtime stories. Only for those stories, they leave out the guts and the gore.

We'd been playing this dance for far too long now.

And now, I was contemplating cancelling my date with Ashley. If I'd known all along that she had the same, if not close to the same, feelings I had been having, I never would've even spoken to the chick in the store.

My thoughts were running rampant in my mind when her bedroom door opened. It wasn't that I'd heard her boots stomping on the floor. It was almost as if I could sense her coming. When I glanced over my shoulder at her, I was knocked on my ass.

"You look nice, Kitten," I mumbled. She looked better than nice. I never kept my mouth closed when it meant something. But for some reason I'd kept my mouth shut.

Good god, she was gorgeous.

Something about all the innocence that seemed to wrap itself around her was as toxic as a drug. To say I was addicted was an understatement.

She had on jeans that hugged her luscious thighs like a vise grip, not to mention she had on a pretty cashmere sweater. How did I know that's what it was called? Because that's what she told me that day I'd taken her out shopping to the superstore. The moment she had walked from the dressing room, I'd been instantly hard.

What further did it for me at that moment was that she styled her hair like the way she had worn it before to a barbeque when I'd made the comment that I loved it like that.

It was braided on the top part only and pulled up into a ponytail, she had told me that it was a faux hawk but for girls with long hair. Hell, I didn't give a damn if it was called a twist or anything like that, it looked great on her.

"Thanks." She smiled at me, but I noticed the sadness. "What about you? You clean up very nice." All I had on was a button-down shirt and clean jeans.

"Kitten, this ain't me cleaning up."

"Oh? Then what do you call this look?"

"It's the look of I don't really want to do this, but it'll be good for me. About time I did start settling down." But it wasn't with the woman that I had the date with.

Ever since that conversation, images of what Novalie would look like barefoot and pregnant assaulted me, not to mention how she would look walking down the aisle in a wedding dress and only having eyes for me.

"Kane, I . . ." I wished she would have been able to finish whatever she was about to say. If she would've said that she really wanted my answer to her confession, by god, I was going to give it to her. But a knock sounded at our door.

Growling in frustration I stalked over to the door like a possessive lion wanting to protect his queen. But I had moves to plan and make. I grabbed the door handle and yanked it open, looking at the punk-ass who was there to take my Kitten out for a night on the town.

"Ah, hey, I'm looking for Novalie," he stammered out.

Son of a bitch. I didn't want to let my Kitten go out with this punk-ass kid. He had on jeans that hugged his legs. He doesn't have a goddamn dick. Don't even get me started on the wrinkled as fuck t-shirt. That wasn't how you took a girl, no scratch that, a woman like Novalie out to dinner.

"Yeah, Cal, I'm here." She smiled at him. It wasn't the smile that she gave to me. Well at least there was that. It wasn't her megawatt smile.

"Cool. Uh, you ready?" He's seriously not going to compliment her. The fact that she of all people had chosen this limp dick to take her out . . .

"Yeah," she said to him. "Have a nice night, Cotton." And there it was, the damn bullet that hit the dam and allowed it to fucking crack wide the fuck open.

Cotton. Not Kane.

I did this. I should've told her how I felt. Well, she better enjoy her night with the punk ass because tonight, I was claiming what's been rightfully mine since day one.

First, I had to deal with Ashley, take her ass to dinner, and then get back home. Second, I was going to make it known that Novalie was mine.

She had told me that she saw me more than a father figure, more than a guardian, more than a brother or even an uncle. Why the fuck hadn't I answered her instead of being a dick? Yet here I was still kicking my own ass as I locked the house and went to my bike, then my phone went off and it was my date for the evening. Yeah, I was running late but fuck.

I hadn't been on a date in almost three years. Was this really a date? Two people grabbing a bite to eat? With someone that I really don't even like? Or was it that I just needed to get laid and I knew she was easy?

Yet I still didn't know why I'd agreed to go on this date. Maybe I was hard up and just really needing some action. That was the only reason, well, that had been the only reason until earlier today.

I didn't appreciate the fact that when I knocked on her door, she was in a hot pink mini skirt and a top that looked like her damn tits were about to pop out.

"You got on shorts under that skirt? We're taking the bike." The look of horror was clearly etched all over her caked-up face. Thank fuck it wasn't my everyday bike, but one I needed to get out of the shed and run so I could sell it. It was collecting dust.

Whenever Novalie dressed in sweatpants, a tank, and a messy bun, with a clean face all void of makeup, it was all I could do to keep my hands from roaming her body, seeing if her skin felt as soft as it looked.

However, a woman looking like Ashley right now, I just realized I'd been blind my whole damn life. I preferred Novalie's natural look over anything.

"No! I bought this outfit especially for our date! Besides, you're late." Well, she looked offended if I were to judge that based on the fact that she had cocked her small ass waist and placed her hand on her hip. I really didn't give a fuck.

"You knew me when you asked me out. I ain't no different now than I was a few days ago. Bike or nothing at all. I run an MC, Ashley. I'm going to be late. That can't be helped"

"I know that, Cotton. But I've also had my eye on you for a while now."

"Yeah?" I barely even knew the bitch except for the time I'd declined the dinner invitation. She had come to the clubhouse for some of the open parties we had, but that was it.

"We can take my car," she purred. When she ran her hand down my chest, my entire body tightened. "I've got a surprise for you. Easy access tonight. I'm not wearing any panties. You know you want this." She purred yet again, trying to be seductive.

It took all I had to not grab her by the wrist and twist until she figured it out, she didn't need to touch me. But it wasn't that. Her touch wasn't Novalie's.

"Yeah, this ain't going to work." I'd had enough. I turned at her door and marched back to my bike.

"Cotton, what did I do?" she yelled after me.

I was fed up beating around the bush. I wanted my Kitten, and I wasn't waiting until tonight. She had laid her cards there on the table for the whole world to see. I was hers.

I called Dale, and he answered on the second ring, "Yeah, Pres."

"Get me a location on Novalie."

She had the nerve to call me Cotton when I was Kane to her? We were going to have that conversation too.

"Yeah, just second." I heard typing which meant Dale was in his geek room, as we all called it.

"I don't understand. I'll go put on jeans if that's what you want." When had Ashley come down her porch stairs?

I heard Dale chuckling through the phone

"Ashley, you're not what I want." When she opened her mouth to protest, I continued, "And you'll never be what I want." I looked at her. "Now, you bother me again, you'll find out why I'm the President of one of the biggest MC's on the east coast." I didn't give a fuck if it sounded callous or was mean. It was honest. And that's all I ever claimed to be.

"Got it. She's at Alexandro's." I hung up the phone, started the bike, and headed for Alexandro's.

Boy was trying to get in her fucking pants. Not today, boy, in fact not ever.

Normally, that drive would be a good half an hour, but I made it in twenty minutes. I pulled my bike right in front of the door. Was I supposed to park there? Nope. Did I give a damn? Again, nope. Was I coming out alone? Hell fucking no.

So, she needed an easy walk out of the building, and a ride at the curb waiting for her? I got that.

After I took my helmet off and swung from my bike, some pimple-faced dick was stammering at me, telling me that I couldn't park there. I didn't even give the man a second glance as I pushed past him.

When I entered the semi-dark lit room, the hostess asked if I had a reservation. Shaking her off, I scanned the restaurant.

And there was my Kitten, sitting at a table for two across from the little punk ass kid. I heard her whisper-yell at him that she wanted more than a salad. And when I heard the fucker say that she apparently needed to eat only salads, my fury skyrocketed. It wasn't just me who heard that. It was the whole damn restaurant.

I stalked to their table, and as if she felt me coming this time, she turned her head just as her eyes lit up like I was her savior. When I got to her, I placed one hand on the back of her chair and one hand on the table in front of her. Then I leaned down and kissed her forehead.

"Kitten," I whispered. Her eyelids did a slight droop at my tone.

"Kane," she whispered back.

I turned my head to look at the kid. "Next time you take a girl out to dinner, when you pick her up, you compliment her on what she's wearing when you first lay eyes on her. Second, you don't show up to her house in a wrinkled-up t-shirt for a damn date. And third, you never order for her and you don't order her a damn salad. You order her a damn steak and a baked potato because, boy, there ain't nothing sexier on a woman than fucking curves for a man to grab hold of. And lastly, when you have a woman on a date with you, your eyes stay trained on her, period." When I finished, I turned my head back to my Kitten.

"Can I take you somewhere, feed you, then take you home and really show you my feelings for you?" When she inhaled deeply and nodded slightly, I straightened, pulled my wallet from my back pocket, and threw down a twenty.

"For my woman's meal." Then I offered her my hand as she stood.

The moment she was facing me, I let go of all the 'should not's. I gave into my emotions, wrapped one hand around the back of her neck, then I brought my mouth down on hers.

It wasn't a passionate kiss, nor was it a 'fuck you' kiss. No, it was a claiming kiss, and when she opened her mouth for me to slide my tongue in? That was the other game-changer.

After a few seconds, I pulled away from her. Judging by the way her eyes were half-lidded over, she was unsteady, and then she beamed that smile at me. My megawatt smile.

"Let's go, Kitten." She threw her head back and laughed as we strode from the restaurant hand-in-hand as rounds of claps and laughter followed us out.

When Novalie had her helmet on, I looked over at DeMarco, the cop in Clearwater, and smirked. DeMarco just turned his lights off, shook his head, and drove off.

I took her to a little mom-and-pop joint that was about twenty minutes away. Thankfully, it was only eight and I knew the owners.

Before we got off the bike, I placed my hand on her thigh.

"Kitten, I'm going to say this one time and one time only. You listen, yeah?"

"Yeah, Kane." I closed my eyes at the way her voice sounded when she said my name.

"You and me, we're a thing. Means I'm yours and you're mine. Not my ole' lady yet because I'm giving you time to come to terms with what being with me means, yeah?"

"Yeah, Kane. Now, I like you a lot too, but please feed me something more than a salad," she stated, and that caused a laugh to erupt from my mouth.

A sound that was very rare for me, and it felt good.

As we walked hand-in-hand again with hers fitting perfectly into my much larger one, I chose a booth that was near to the back wall. I smirked when she sat in the one closest to the wall just as I slid in after her.

"Well, as I live and breathe. Cotton, good to see you." There was the man who allowed me to work in the back under the table to help my grandfather and keep me out of trouble in my younger years before the garage and the MC was even a dream.

"Wes, it's good to see you. This is my woman, Novalie. Novalie, this is Wes, a good friend of mine." When she smiled at Wes, I saw Wes's eyes crinkle. Yeah, she had that effect on people.

Snorting, I said, "Give us two of your specials."

"Do you think you're just going to order your food from me and not tell me about the beautiful woman sitting beside you?"

"Wes, she's mine. Kitten, this is Wes. He owns this place. He helped keep me out of trouble during my younger years. There, is that better?" I asked Wes. Fucking troublemaker.

"Oh yeah? Do you have any stories?" my Kitten asked.

"A woman after my own heart. Girl, I could give you stories about our boy here that would curl your toes." And then a look crossed over her face, and it was one that caused a heat to fire up deep in my veins.

"On second thought, Wes, how about you make that order to go?" I asked as I was still looking at Novalie and the hooded expression over her eyes told me that she wanted me just as badly as I wanted her.

It took ten minutes for the food to be ready and we were out the door.

"Do come back when you have more time." Wes had called after us. The little fucker was laughing his ass off. Yes, I was being led by my dick, but have you looked at her? Enough said.

As soon as I pulled the Harley into the garage, I had my helmet off, I grabbed her body up and off my bike, giving her time to take her helmet off while she was in my arms. Then I carried her into the house and down the hall to my bedroom.

Setting her down on her feet, I warned, "Kitten, you don't want this, now is the time to tell me. And be honest with me because I won't be able to hold back once we start."

And in response, per usual of my Kitten, she stood on her tiptoes, placed her hands on either side of my face, looked deeply into my eyes before she closed hers, then brought her mouth up to mine.

And it was the sweetest, softest kiss I had ever experienced in my life. That was enough for me. I tilted her head back even more as I delved deeper into her mouth with my tongue.

That was liquid fire.

However, she pulled away too soon for my liking. "Kane, before we go any further. You should know that I haven't been with a man, as in ever." If that didn't solidify the fact that she was made for me, then I didn't really know what would.

"Kitten, that's the sweetest thing a woman can give a man. To know I'm your first and your last, god damn, Kitten." I growled.

She lazily began to take my clothes off. The first thing to go had been my kutte, which she took and hung it on the door knob, then my shirt was next. So, I began stripping off her clothes piece by piece, when I stepped out of my pants, I allowed her to take in everything that was now hers.

"Your tatts are a masterpiece, Kane." When Novalie leaned forward and kissed a scar just above my rib cage that had been covered, my skin tingled all over.

I kissed her again, loving just how her touch calmed the raging war that played constantly in my head. I wanted to explore her whole body, not be some rushed, frenzied affair, but the more she touched me, skin to skin, I was vastly losing control.

Still I tried to take my time as I worshipped her body. I didn't want this to ever be a regret for her.

"Kane, I feel . . . I feel like my whole body is on fire."

"And?" I asked her in between lavishing her breasts that fit my hands perfectly. As I worked my way down her body, in between movements, I asked, "Do . . . you . . . like it?"

If all she could manage was a head nod, I would take that.

"Do me a favor, don't ever get this pierced?" I loved the way her stomach was taut and lean, simple.

"Yes, Kane." I doubted she even understood what she was agreeing to at this moment. Her eyes were closed—oh, that would not do.

"Kitten, eyes open, babe. Wanna watch you come apart."

She opened her eyes, the passion she felt was clearly written in those deep blue orbs. "Hurry, Kane, I need . . . I need . . ."

"Tell me, Kitten, what do you need?"

"I need . . . this feeling . . . I'm burning inside," she withered underneath my fingertips.

So, I relieved that burning with my mouth. I took in her perfect pussy, it smelled fucking heavenly. With a few long, leisurely licks, I could practically feel her body trembling and beginning to hum. I flattened my tongue on her clit and stroked until she came apart, screaming my name.

She nearly busted out my ear drums. "Kane!" she yelled. "Oh, Kane!"

As I got on top of her, I readied my dick at her entrance. I felt so fucking sorry for the pain that I was about to cause her, but I would make a world of difference for her in a bit.

"You ready, Kitten?"

"Kane, please. You doused that fire, but it's raging again. Hurry, Kane."

This was the one time that I knew I was going to deny her, and truth be told, it ate me up inside.

With my gaze never leaving hers, I made my way inside of her, inch by inch, until I felt her hymen and I stopped. I waited for her to get used to the size of me inside of her.

And just like that, not once had she closed her eyes.

"Ready, Kane." Yes, she was but first, we had a score to settle.

"Kitten, we will not have this conversation again. If you ever call me Cotton again, I will be withholding my dick from you. You call me Kane." Cotton would never sound right coming from her mouth ever again.

"Yes, Kane. Now, please," she begged. She would never have to beg me for a goddamn thing. All that I have to give is hers already.

Leaning my head down I kissed her hard as I pushed the rest of the way in, feeling her body tighten at the intrusion, but I hoped like hell this was at least helping her.

I was finally fucking home.

Fuck, I was already needing to come. "God damn, Kitten, you're so fucking tight," I breathed out.

"Kane, move." Novalie had her legs wrapped around my waist.

"Kitten, yeah." So, I moved. With each stroke, though I didn't think it was possible, her walls got tighter.

"Kane!" she yelled as I stroked the inside of her walls. Thrusting in and out of her was fucking heaven.

I never understood the saying about if it was my time, then this was the way to go. But now, I did. I finally understand what it means to feel perfect. I was feeling perfect right fucking now.

Breathing in through my nose, out through my mouth, I had to hold myself back from coming.

"Kane . . . I need to . . . I'm going to . . ."
Knowing what she needed I fingered her clit, as her eyes widened and her cheeks flushed, she's never looked more beautiful.

"Yeah, Kitten, let go, babe. Come with me." I ground out, as soon as I felt her body spasm and felt her calves tighten, I knew her toes had just curled too.

It was then that I felt my spine tingle just as I felt her release, I allowed myself to cum with her.

The look on her face was a work of fucking art. God himself broke the mold when he made her. She had always been beautiful, but in that moment after she came, she was fucking gorgeous.

For the first time in my whole entire life, I didn't just fuck someone. No, I made love to her.

We made love that night, she gave me the most precious gift a woman can give a man, that being something that I would forever be grateful for. And now, I was going to make damn sure that I would be forever deserving to be the man she chose.

Thankfully, I knew I had done my job right after three times of making love because after I left the bathroom from cleaning up, a light soft snore was coming from the bed. My Kitten was fast asleep with all of her hair splayed over my pillows.

Smiling a rare smile, I cleaned her up then tossed the washcloth into the hamper, once I gathered her close, I fell asleep.

I didn't dream about the lives that I had ended. I didn't dream about the friends I've lost. No, I dreamt about a little boy that was just like me, and a beautiful little girl that would be just like her momma.

Chapter 8

'Good southern peaches, baby.'

Novalie

When I awoke that next morning, for the first time I really dreaded going into work. It wasn't the customers or having to work that was starting to get to me. No, it was my manager.

The past few months, things had really started to get crazy at work. August, September, and October had all been filled with the same drama. I was so close to finding somewhere else to work.

Deidra had been recently hired so that Virginia could take some time off with her husband. I respected the chain of command and all that, but there was only so much one person could take.

Deidra, the manager, took a special dislike to me, and at first, I had no idea why. It wasn't until apparently Deidra had told another one of the waitresses, Fiona, why she hated me. All the while I'd been standing around the corner at the small set of lockers in the storage room, where we all stowed our stuff.

I knew Deidra didn't appreciate the way Cotton had looked at me when he came in on my later shifts, and that was because Deidra wanted him to look at her the same way.

And now, any time one of the customers got rowdy with me, instead of Deidra stepping in like she did with the other waitresses, she left me hanging out to dry. Cotton told me that I should take it to Virginia. But Virginia had enough on her plate to deal with than arguing females who just didn't get along.

So instead, I snuggled deeper into Cotton, knowing I would more than likely be late, but this was so worth it.

"Morning, Kitten." It was an amazing feeling, that moment when your dream turned into a reality.

And then it hit me—oh god, my breath. I needed to brush my teeth. So, imagine my horror when I tried to get out of bed to do just that and his steel band of an arm tightened down around my hips. It would seem I wasn't going anywhere until he was ready to release me.

"Where you going?" Even his voice, all sleepy, caused that fire to sizzle in my veins.

"To brush my teeth," I said with my hand covering my mouth.

"Kitten, you will not leave this bed without a good morning to me and after you give me that mouth." It was another side of him that he was letting me see. My own big MC President being a gooey marshmallow.

I struggled that little bit, but took the plunge and said, "Good morning." And then I gave him my mouth.

He, however, was immune to my morning breath, as evident by the moan that escaped his mouth when our tongues had entwined as they danced their own rhythm.

However, one thing led to another and then we ended up making love.

But before I walked out the door to go to work, I turned at the door as he was watching me from over the rim of his cup of coffee.

"Kane, thank you. Thank you for making me very happy." I didn't realize this was only the start of my forever.

"Kitten, you ain't the only one." With a brow lift, he gifted me with his dimpled smile.

So, to my horror, when I walked into Virginia's half an hour late for my shift, a round of laughter came from the women, all but Deidra.

"You've got that glow, girlie. Cotton do right by you?" Virginia was a mother to us all.

"We are so not discussing this," I rattled off with a chuckle.

Then a rattle of laughter followed me to the back, where I donned my apron and got to work.

As a favor to Virginia, I pulled a double and that night while I was on shift, I saw two men at the counter with Deidra hunched over the diner top. All of a sudden, the hairs on the back of my nape began to tingle and raise. Whenever that happened, something was about to go seriously wrong.

Thankfully, Walker had been placed in the back corner in regular clothes so as to not draw attention to himself, as ordered by Cotton. Normally it was Xavier that was my shadow but Cotton needed him at the clubhouse tonight.

This had been the case ever since I'd moved in with him and more so when I told him about what was going down at the diner. I rarely went anywhere without someone watching out for me unless I was working.

And today, I was grateful. I also knew that from his angle, he couldn't see the backs of the men.

I made my way to the back corner and talked to Walker, who was here today instead of Xavier.

"Walker, I need you to call Cotton, now." I knew I wasn't supposed to speak to the brothers that way, but I couldn't shake this eerie feeling. And judging by what was on the backs of the two men at the counter, I was right in doing so.

I didn't see a look of spite or hatred for speaking to him like that. It was more of a respectful look and a non-judging look. That was new.

"Yeah, Pres? Novalie needs to talk to you." He handed the phone to me.

"Kane?"

"Yeah, Kitten? Everything okay?" There was a hint of worry there in his voice. I'd not had a reason to call him while I'd been at work. Anytime I needed to talk to him, I just texted.

"Kane, I'm not sure if this matters now, but there are a couple guys from the Spades MC in here at the diner. They're bent low over the counter, whispering to Deidra," I said low into the phone, and from my angle, they couldn't see me, but I had a direct line of view on them.

His response was instant.

"Grab your stuff and hand the phone back to the prospect." To anyone else, he would've appeared to have been cool and collected, only I knew better.

I walked as calmly as I could to my locker and grabbed my things. Thankfully, no one was the wiser.

After living with him for almost six months now, I have come to a point where I know more about a man who isn't a relative than I do about my own mother.

After Cotton had banned my parents from the club almost five months ago, they hadn't returned, nor had they called to check in on me.

It took only a second for Cotton to speak to the prospect before a look of foreboding hit his face.

"Here, keep this to your ear. Let's go," he whispered in my ear, so no one would pick up on the unrest we were both feeling.

As I followed the prospect from the back door and mounted the bike, I had Cotton in my ear.

"Kitten, I need you to hold on as tight as you can," It sounded like he was running, and I could hear him shouting out orders.

"Okay, Kane." As we peeled away from the parking lot, I heard two other motors start-up and tires screeching as we made a right turn.

"Kane, I think they know we left," I yelled into the phone.

It was then that he began to shout even more orders.

I heard him telling everyone to grab their piece and make their way to the blacktop.

"Kane, they're shooting at us," I yelled into the phone as I could feel the power of the bullets literally zinging past us as glass from cars were being shattered.

I didn't let on, but I felt something scrape my right thigh. It hurt like a mother, but there was no time for whining, not when literally, our lives depended on making it to the clubhouse safely.

"Tell Prospect to hurry the fuck up. I ain't losing you," he growled.

Then, like he had supersonic hearing, Walker sped even faster. Thankfully, Cotton had shown me how to hold on and lean with the turns or else we would've been in a ditch somewhere knocking on heaven's door.

Within minutes, the clubhouse was in view and I could see the entire club lined up on the blacktop. A few of them were on their bikes, revving up their engines as if gearing up to ride out after them.

We kept going, and at the last minute, Walker throttled down so we could make the turn and not end up as vulture food. Then we were in the safety of the clubhouse and the guys on the bikes rode after the two men.

Shots were being fired outside the compound, and after an insane amount of yelling, the shots had ceased.

The moment the bike stopped, I climbed off as soon as Walker did and looked for Cotton. The exact moment I had him in my sights, I took off and let my feet carry my body, my heart, and my soul.

When I got into jumping distance, I launched myself at him, he didn't even have to step back to catch me. Talk about freaking awesome. I never wanted to leave his arms.

"Kane." I was trying so hard to keep the tears at bay that wanted to sail from my eyes like a river and be the woman he needed me to be. With my face buried in his neck, he walked us over to the clubhouse as I breathed him in to calm my raging emotions.

"Kitten, you're safe. I've got you. Are you hurt?" I loved that whenever he had been away from me for too long, he almost always checked me over to make sure I was whole.

"No," I murmured into his neck. I didn't tell him about my thigh, not when he had more important matters to see to.

After a few moments, I relaxed my hold on him and lowered my legs. As soon as my right leg touched back down on the pavement, it took everything in me to not let out a wince.

He kept his hand on the back of my neck and luckily hadn't seen anything. He wrapped his other hand around my waist.

He moved my hair off one shoulder and then placed a kiss behind my ear. That also seemed to be the new move that he changed to. He still kissed my forehead, but the behind the ear thing was new.

"Go inside, Kitten. I've got to take care of this."

"Okay, Kane," I said, then turned and gave a smile to all of the brothers and especially to Walker for what they had done for me. "Walker, thank you."

"No problem, darlin'." It was comical when his face turned to ash as he then looked at Cotton.

"Call her that again regardless of if you are a brother, and I'll hang you from your goddamn balls." Cotton was jovial maybe two times out of ten, and the other eight times, he was one alpha male.

Walker's mouth dropped and he began stammering, trying to backtrack. "Yes, Pres. Sorry."

I was so on the verge of screaming at Cotton telling him that I loved him, but that was for us to experience alone. Plus, I hoped with everything in me that those feelings will be returned tenfold.

Then it was his actions that showed me that I was possibly right. He leaned down, kissed my forehead yet again then left me standing there to head to the shed.

Where I had seen Garret and Knox pulling the two men in tow, the shed where I knew a lot of blood had more or less been spilled.

So, I did the only thing that I could really do to help as I made my way into the clubhouse and sought Lucy. Lucy was also a retired nurse.

Not seeing her in the common room, I made my way into the kitchen. Seeing as it was about time for the girls to cook for the brothers who lived at the clubhouse, I intended to help.

"Hey, Novalie." Lucy smiled as I entered.

"Hey, Lucy. Can I borrow you for a second?" Lucy followed me to the bathroom.

"Can you look at my leg and check it out?" I winced when I grazed the wound.

"Novalie," Lucy whispered, knowing good and well that if Cotton knew I was hurt, I wouldn't be on my feet right now.

Once we got my leggings off, Lucy peered at the area. It was marked, but it wasn't bleeding or anything. How in the world had that happened?

She told me that sometimes a bullet can barely graze your skin and it can leave a mark like that. Thankfully, the bullet wasn't any closer or else it would have done some damage.

"Your leg will probably be sore for a day or two. Take aspirin if you need it."

With a nod to me, Lucy left the bathroom and allowed me to finish dressing back up.

As soon as I reentered the kitchen, I asked, "Need any help?"

"Yeah, can you dice up those potatoes?" Lucy was making mashed potatoes. Lucy's potatoes were the bomb.

"You got it," I said as I went toward the cutting board and the potatoes.

"Well, if it isn't another biker whore we have to contend with." Some brunette Jolie wannabe said as she walked into the kitchen.

"Amberly, no. She's Cotton's," Vas scolded the Amberly woman when she walked in behind me.

"Cotton's whore? She's still just a whore." Instantly, I had a serious dislike for this woman.

"You disrespect her like that in front of me again, I'll show you why my knuckles don't bleed anymore," Vas warned as she stared at Amberly.

Lucy sat her knife down and looked at her. "Amberly, you're barking up the wrong tree here, best you leave her alone."

"Lucy, I ain't got no beef with you. You're an ole' lady." I could tell it was taking all that Lucy had in her to not say more, but I knew this was boiling up and it was my fight to have.

"No disrespect when I'm talking to a whore though." Before Vas could bring her arm up and do anything, I halted her.

"Vas, it's okay," I told her. I really liked that Vas had my back.

"Yeah, you're okay with me calling you a whore because you are one," the woman said snidely.

"I'm not one to throw small punches or start a cat fight, but last time I checked, being with more than one man meant you were a whore. But I make special exceptions to that rule. I only see one whore in this room, and that's you." No way would I ever call Vas or Greta, another club girl, a whore. Yes, they slept with the brothers, but they also knew their limits with the ladies, and they respected them.

I judged them by how they had treated me.

"You're no better than me," Amberly said.

"Well, considering I can count how many men I've been with on one hand and on one finger, what does that make you?" I asked her, but I had apparently been talking to deaf ears. I hadn't noticed the figure that had moved into the kitchen.

Then, a look of shock marred Amberly's ugly face. "You're walking a very thin fucking line," a dangerous voice said from the doorway, and that belonged to a pissed-off Cotton.

"I didn't mean anything by it. Just a friendly—" Amberly started to say.

I couldn't help the snort that slipped out.

Cotton's face was scaring all the women in the room. I saw that they all had gathered behind me as if I were their human shield, being that Cotton would never harm me.

"You even look wrong in her direction again, you're fucking gone. I don't give a goddamn what my brothers think of your overused pussy. You got me?" Cotton said in a tone so low, my lady bits did a little tingle.

"Yes, Cotton," Amberly muttered.

"Now, get the fuck in there and help instead of acting like you're someone's ole' lady," Cotton had grumbled.

And then, he sauntered over toward me.

"First of all, wanna tell me why you didn't tell me you hurt your leg? Second, why are you even in here helping? That's not your job, Kitten." Every single time he treated me with the utmost care, I wanted to scream from the rooftops that I loved him. But now wasn't the right time either.

"Kane, I'm fine. Really. The mark on my leg is just that, a mark. And I'm not an ole' lady, Kane, therefore, I help. Besides, I owe Vas a beer." And I loved that he allowed himself to softly laugh in front of me but also in front of the other women.

I watched as that small smile of his dimmed into a tense line.

"No, you're not an ole' lady, yet, but you are my Kitten." That right there was more proof that he possibly loved me back.

"That's right, I am your Kitten, but I do owe Vas a beer," I said.

"Well, allow me." A quick kiss and he was gone from the kitchen, only to return with two ice-cold beers.

"Thank you, honey." I leaned up on my tip-toes and kissed him for all I was worth.

"I'm sorry, Novalie, I didn't know," Amberly told me after Cotton left the kitchen. I got it, though. I had also seen the look on Amberly's face when she heard me call him Kane and not Cotton.

For the most part, that seemed to do it with everyone. Thankfully.

I had talked to Vas one afternoon and had learned that in other clubs, if a club girl didn't make it known that she was strong, then she was walked all over. And in other clubs, it didn't matter if a man was taken or not, the club girls still had the right to get their paws on them.

But not Wrath MC. If a brother chose a woman for his ole' lady, then he didn't wander. It was also one of their most sacred laws. If a brother was found to be cheating on his ole' lady with a club girl, then that brother got a beatdown.

And it was worse if an ole' lady was found cheating. She would disappear and then her name would be blacklisted from being mentioned within or even outside of the club.

"We're cool, but don't disrespect another one of the ladies regardless of who or what they are. We're outnumbered. The last thing we need is for the women to be catty and make this whole club sour. Now, if someone who isn't club comes in here and tries to start shit, feel free to lay the bitch on her ass. Because I'll help," I said with a smile on my face.

"Same," Vas and Greta both agreed at the same time and so had Lucy with a nod of her head.

"Yeah, you're right. What can I do to help?" Amberly's tone had changed drastically.

So, with the five of us working we had meatloaf, mashed potatoes, macaroni n cheese, a green bean casserole, and rolls for all the men.

After everyone had their bellies full, and all the food was demolished, a thought occurred to me. As soon as I watched him enter his office, I had my mind made up.

I was going to give my man one of my fantasies. I was going to drop to my knees and bring him pleasure.

Naughty style.

Chapter 9

'Let me be your fantasy.'

Cotton

"Kitten, I've got church to get to, what are you doing?" If there was one thing within my club, it was that a law was never meant to be broken. You were never late for church. Not unless you had a damn good reason or explicit consent from me. That even applied to myself.

However, the moment I saw the spark in her eyes, I knew. I was about to find out exactly what that look had been all about.

As she made her way to me, I had to bite back the growl of arousal. Damn her.

"Something I want to try. I need you to have an open mind. Something that I've never done before," she murmured as she began to unbutton my jeans.

"Kitten, office door is wide the fuck open." If she were about to do what I thought she was, there was no way in hell that anyone was going to see that side of her.

"Okay," she said as she worked her hand inside my jeans, moved my boxers out of her way, and then she pulled my dick out.

She pushed me back until my ass hit my leather chair and she smiled as she knelt in front of me and placed her hands on my thighs.

At her moan, the traitorous fucker definitely showed that it wanted it's woman too. I was at full mast already and she hadn't even done a damn thing to me yet.

When she brought out her tongue and touched the tip of my cock, I felt pre-cum leak out of the head.

Then, as if she had no inhibitions, she pulled me into her mouth, full hilt, all the fucking way to the back of her throat. She swirled her tongue around and around my shaft, working it in and out of her mouth.

What was about to push me over the edge was that I felt her throat muscles. My woman didn't have a fucking gag reflex. It was in that exact moment that I realized the door was still standing wide the fuck open and I just didn't have it in me to care.

"Kitten, you don't want me to come in your mouth, you pull back now and use your hand." My voice rasped as I struggled to get those few words out.

As if I was just like a teenage boy with his first-ever pussy I came. A full fucking load. What had sent me soaring over the edge had been when she had moaned and renewed in her vigor letting me know that I wasn't leaving her mouth until I gave her what she wanted.

"Tasted freaking sweet, honey," she purred at me, licking her lips in the process.

With that she stood, tossed a wink over her shoulder as she turned and strode from my office, all the while leaving my dick hanging out in the wide fucking open.

Once I put my dick back in place, zipped up my jeans, I stood and strode from my office out into the hall with the biggest fucking grin I could muster. The moment my brothers saw my expression, booming laughter broke out around the table in church.

"Guess we can forgive you for being late to church, old man," York stammered out between laughs.

"For real, you making her your ole' lady?" Garret asked.

That was an odd question coming from Garret.

"Ain't none of your damn business." I damn sure didn't like the way Garret was looking at me either. Sure, was it my business when one of them were thinking about it? Yes. But not them asking me.

"Well, guess I'm making it my business. She's good with my daughter. Not to mention she's easy on the eyes too." The fucker was lucky I considered him more than a brother.

"Yeah? You keep going on with that way of thinking and I'll put a bullet right between your eyes." I wasn't fooling around either. Novalie was mine and mine she would stay.

"Yeah, that's what I thought." An all-knowing smile spread across Garret's face and the same with all my brothers.

"Enough of this pussy shit. Since when did one-percenter MC bikers act like a bunch of fucking women?" I asked the room as a whole, still many of them wore smiles.

"Alright, we got a lead on Amy and French. Sanchez owes me a favor. I'm calling in that marker to see what the fuck has really been going on."

"I got a feeling he knows more than what he's been saying," Dale said from his corner in the room.

"Well, considering it ain't much, that's not saying a whole lot." That came from Cooper, who was sitting to the left of York. He wasn't lying about that.

For some reason, after Sanchez had stopped me in the street, we'd also not had any more runs that had gotten fucked with.

After we had gone around the table and discussed any matters we needed to discuss, we brought our attention to the other project at hand.

"York, how did the new girl get to her location?" I asked.

"Well, the dumb bitch didn't believe us when we told her she couldn't take anything from her old life. She took an old phone that she said she had a few pictures on. That phone was still active." Of course, it was.

"And therefore, easy to track," Dale said at a murmur.

"Yeah, he found her while they were out on the road, but Powers had a man on her that her douchebag of an ex didn't factor in. That man being Heathen."

"Hot damn, that son of a bitch—Well, other than you, Pres—is one man that I don't ever want to be put in a cage with again. Damn near killed me the last time I faced off with him. I think since he doesn't talk to anyone nor allows himself to be touched it gives him more power." Garret was one strong fuck, and it took a lot for him to admit that.

Knox nodded from the end of the table as well.

Hell, I was able to attest to that statement too. Heathen was one scary fuck. But also so was Skinner, another member of our Dogwood Chapter. He just didn't fight, but his scars. That showed a side of him that he hadn't delved to the world.

"Good. So, she's safe now?"

"Yeah, I checked in with her this morning. Said she was really liking her new digs and she wanted to say thank you," Cooper muttered from his chair though.

"Alright, and last but not least, bring Xavier in here," I told the room.

We waited for Cooper to regain his seat and for Xavier to close the door.

"Okay, so it's that time where we vote on whether we're going to let a prospect join us. As you all know that vote has to be unanimous. We're voting on Xavier. All in agreement, let me hear you." And as if it had been planned, no one said a damn thing.

Everyone was looking at Xavier and we could see the sweat rolling down his forehead. The man was trying to stay stoic, but his nerves were eating him alive.

Then all of a sudden, a round of "fuck yes" filled the space. A sheer look of amazement assaulted Xavier's face.

"Get your kutte to Lucy. She'll sew your new patches on for you," I told him.

"Thanks, Pres. Thanks, boys." You could hear how emotional Xavier was just from the sound of his voice.

"Move your shit into French's old room. Hell, it isn't like he's going to need it," I said in a dark sarcastic voice.

With that being the end of church, I slammed the gavel back down and headed out to find my Kitten.

But first, the men had rounds of shots for celebratory drinks. A patch-in party would be in the air in the next few days.

"Yeah?" I answered my phone when I saw Walker's name pop up.

"Pres, not sure this is a good thing, but thought you ought to know. Novalie and her friend, June, are looking at apartments. Last time I checked, June had a place and Novalie is with you," Walker had said over the phone.

Normally, I had Xavier on Novalie, but Xavier had to be there today to be voted in or out. Walker had been out on duty today, and after he showed promise after the ordeal in the diner, I'd assigned that detail to Walker.

But first, I needed to know why the fuck she was out looking for somewhere else to live, seeing as I thought I'd made my intentions known more times than I had cared to really admit.

That night, however, after she had finished saying her piece, she looked at me and that look in her eyes that I'd been trying to decipher for quite a while now was clear as fuck to me.

All she was doing was preparing for a future without me if she had to. Normally, a strong and confident woman scared men off. But those men weren't me and I found that trait sexy as fuck.

Now, the only thing I had to do was get her to tell me first that she loved me. No way in hell was I admitting that shit first.

Chapter 10

'Love conquers all.'

Novalie

Our conversation a few days ago played over in my mind like it was on a record player set to one track and one track only.

He didn't get upset when he had called me to see where I was and when I told him over the phone that I was out looking at apartments with June, he still didn't sound upset.

And he still didn't get upset when I told him that I was grabbing dinner with June and that I would be back at his house in about an hour or so.

Also, to my delight, June and I talked the other day and we'd gotten down to what was really going on with her. She didn't want to tell me that she had changed her mind on going to nursing school with me.

No matter the reason, I couldn't wait for her to come to the clubhouse and hang out with me more. I needed my best friend back.

So that night, to my horror then to my delight, I had walked into his house, he was poised and ready for a talk. A talk where he talked and I listened, then I followed that by agreeing.

The image that he presented showed me all I needed to know. He was bloody furious for some reason. He had a stern look on his face, narrowed eyes, his arms crossed over his chest, and his feet braced a shoulder-width apart against the island that faced the front door.

"Kane . . ."

"First of fucking all, you will tell me where you are going or a general area."

When I moved to speak, he raised an eyebrow, which was code for me to shut up.

"Don't you dare throw me any lip until I've had my say, and if you do throw any lip, I'll put that lip to use babe, and that's a promise."

When I nodded, he continued on, it took all I had to not protest every word from his mouth. I even had to bite my tongue to make sure I kept quiet.

"I want you to at least tell me where you are going or at the very least the general area, so that I know if I ever need to come and get you, or if I need to know the last place you were if something, god forbid, ever happened to you. We've got enemies, babe, and I'm not real keen on losing you. Hell, that is something I don't ever want to think about, because Kitten, you're mine.

Second, did I ask you to move out?" There it was, the reason for his anger.

And before I could open my mouth to respond to him, even though he appeared to be wanting my response, he in fact didn't. He continued on.

"No, I did not ask you to do that. Thought that with the past couple of weeks, with you in my bed and me fucking no, making love to you, and loving that fire that ignites from you as soon as my fingertips touch your skin. And third, don't you ever tell me that this is my house. Babe clue the fuck in yeah. This is our house. And fourth, you want to move somewhere else, then find your forever place and we will move, where you go I, don't matter where, you're my home Kitten."

"Now, I've laid that shit out there, come here and give me your mouth." I stood my ground. I fought the tears that were gathering in the corners of my eyes when he had said that I was his home. He had laid it out there. Now, it was my turn.

"I was looking for an apartment because I didn't want to cramp your style any longer," I said.

"Babe. Come. Here. Now," he growled out.

Yes, sir.

And with that, I didn't mumble that he was bossy, and I didn't give him any lip. No, I freaking melted like a snow cone in the middle of the summer on the beach.

I made her way to him and gave him my mouth.

It was at that moment that I knew without a shadow of a doubt how he really felt; however, I didn't want to focus on the what-ifs. Like what if it hurts when he lets me fall? What if it doesn't mean anything, when I know damn well that it will mean everything to me.

Normally, I wouldn't have believed him when he confessed how much he cared for me like he just did, but his actions showed that he only had eyes for me.

Hell, he had also told me numerous times that if my parents ever showed up anywhere near us again that he was going to take all of the lives from them, tenfold, for all the years they had robbed me of my childhood.

Without a care in the world, he carried me over to the kitchen island. As he laid me down, he stripped me of my clothing as we broke in the kitchen island for the first time.

He ignored the ringing of our phones. He ignored the booming of thunder.

So, after we were finished with round three where we ended up in our bed, and I was wrapped up in his steely arms, I swung for a home run.

"Kane?" Now, this was going to be a conversation where I hoped he wouldn't give me any lip, but that wasn't my Cotton.

"Yeah, Kitten?" he murmured groggily because sleep was vastly approaching him.

"If I were to ever fall, would you catch me?" My breathing sped up as I lay there in anticipation for how he was going to reply, if he even was going to respond at all.

"Kitten, what's this about?" Oh, where to start?

"Well, it's just . . . you know my life hasn't been the greatest. Have I had it rough? Yes. But has it been horrible? No. I've never had someone that I could trust, someone I can call and they're there. But I've never had someone look at me like I was their light in a world full of darkness. So . . . I'll ask again, if I fall, will you catch me?" My breathing slowed.

And what came from his mouth had tears in my eyes instantly.

"Kitten, hope like fuck you're saying you've already fallen." That deep, sexy rasp was in full force tonight, and he didn't sound like his head was still in a cloud of fog either.

And with that, I rolled over in his arms as I buried my face in his neck. In true Cotton fashion in answering, his arms wrapped even tighter around me as I wept silently, not caring one bit if the warm tears wetted our sheets.

This man was my everything.

"I love you." My voice sounded crackled as it murmured against his tanned skin. I hoped that I was able to pour all of my emotions into those three little words that proved it without a shadow of a doubt.

"Kitten, quit crying, you're breaking my heart," he said as he rolled me over onto my back.

And when we were through after the fourth time that night, he wrapped me in his arms once more.

As I was drifting off to sleep, I heard the best four little words I'd ever heard in my life. "Love you too, Kitten."

Then he mumbled into my hair as I finally allowed my eyes to drift closed. "You're my whole world. You knocked those guards down that had been around my heart for the past thirty-six years and you placed yourself within every fiber of my being. Now, go to sleep." He melted me even more, that was my alpha.

"Bossy," I mumbled.

"Babe, yeah."

But I needed to tell him, "Kane, I wanted to—"

"I know. Kitten. Sleep. Now."

"But—" I wished he would let me speak.

"Babe, do I need to fuck you harder to get your mind to close down and go to sleep?" Because that wouldn't be a hardship for me, not at all.

"But Kane, I just wanted to . . ." All I wanted was to tell him thank you for everything he had done for me and he was still continuing to do for me.

"Babe."

And just like that, it was all that was said as I was flipped over onto my stomach, covers array and my undies were then torn from my hips as Cotton entered me in one deft thrust.

"Kane, I liked that pair." And I really freaking did. They were leopard print in a lilac lace color.

"Babe, buy you more tomorrow. Now, enough talk."

So I stopped talking, dug my hands into the covers, and started to meet him thrust for thrust. Every time his cock slid into me, he bottomed out and hit my G-spot every single time. Within minutes I felt my entire body heating with my release that was about to explode.

"I love you, Kane. With everything in me."

And at my words, not only did I come hard as my toes curled, but he also unloaded inside of me growling, "Fucking home. Love the fuck out of you, Kitten."

With that, I smiled like a little canary bird.

After he pulled out of me, he brought a warm wash cloth from the bathroom and cleaned me up. Then I got on my side, threw the covers around me, and as soon as he slid back under the sheets, I covered us both.

Just as his arm banded around me and pulled me into his chest, Cotton whispered, "Fucking beautiful," as his eyelids were lowering, then a soft snore escaped his mouth.

As I thought back to when I'd read a book, it was the hero telling his lady that if she wasn't worn out from their lovemaking, then he didn't do a good enough job.

Well, it would appear that I did a damn good job seeing as her own hero lay there softly snoring against my neck.

Five times in one night would probably wear anyone out, and I had followed shortly after.

***

It was now the day before Thanksgiving, and we were all at the clubhouse preparing the dishes and cleaning up the areas so it would be ready for the masses who were due to hit tomorrow.

We already had the turkeys and the ham seasoned and ready to be put in the oven. The cold dishes were made, the pies were made. The only things left were to peel the potatoes and cook the rest of the dishes.

The beer and liquor run was taken care of, not to mention plenty of Kool-Aid for the kids. This was also the first time that they all came to me for instructions. I went from hardly no one talking to me to following and doing everything I had asked of them.

Thankfully, I also knew that it wasn't pity, nor was it out of duty. But it was out of respect. Respect for Cotton, and respect for me because I had shown them all kindness when some of them never paid me any mind.

That went a long way.

But having Cotton at my back made it all the sweeter.

The next day, we had droves of people showing up. We even had two sister chapters show up for the big feast, including the one Cotton had opened a few weeks ago in South Carolina. Wrath MC really is one great big family.

Sadly, I had tried to get June to come, but she told me she had to work, and she was making double that day.

Just as I was setting out another dish, Fiona, my co-worker from the diner, arrived. Fiona had started to open up to me. What I hadn't realized was that Fiona didn't know exactly how to make friends, since she was a loner, and I had heard that she had no plans for Thanksgiving. That was when I'd invited Fiona.

"So, you know how I told you about watching my grandparents and wanting to find that same kind of love?"

"Yes." We'd both agreed that was the way to go.

"Right, so I was seeing someone. We even got a place together last month. I had been a fool. I walked in and he was banging my sister. All because I wouldn't put out."

"Girl, I've got some men at my back if you want us to go mess him up," I offered freely with a smile.

"Who are we going to mess up?" Xavier asked from over my shoulder.

"I'm going to mess you up, if you keep dropping into my conversations," I told him.

Any time when he was on me, he was notorious for butting his nose in where it didn't belong.

"Yeah, what are you going to do about it? You and your little self." He smirked at me.

Smiling an evil grin, I said, "Kane."

"Yeah, Kitten," he answered me automatically, even though he was halfway across the common room in the clubhouse and was surrounded by the other presidents and the vice presidents.

"I think Xavier here wants to go a round with you in the ring." Take that, punk.

"That right?" he said with a smirk on his all-knowing face, and I received a wink.

"Fuck. Me and my damn mouth," Xavier muttered, I busted out laughing, the whole room erupted in laughter, all of them clapping his back as he walked away from us.

"No, it's okay," she murmured deep into her glass of sweet tea.

Fiona and I had often been mistaken for sisters. We looked that much alike. Our hair was even the same length and near to the same color. Our only difference was that our eyes were different colors. We even wore the same bra size and shoe size. That conversation had occurred over a night of drunken texts.

As I sat there contemplating, I noticed a dark shadow fell over us.

It was Knox. The silent six-foot-seven beast of a man stood there staring at Fiona.

"Knox, this is Fiona. Fiona, this is Knox."

While Knox only had eyes for Fiona, Fiona also only had eyes for Knox.

What I hadn't expected was for him to offer her his hand, and what shocked the heck out of me even further was that Fiona placed her hand in his.

"Who's the asshole I need to go handle?" I heard Knox ask Fiona as he led her away. I was shocked that I had actually heard him say anything, much less eight words.

Turns out I wasn't the only one watching the pair as Knox led Fiona out of the clubhouse and to the back courtyard.

A thought occurred to me that they would make some killer babies, Fiona with her darker color and Knox with his Hispanic features.

I felt the steel arm that belonged to my forever wrap itself around my waist as he pulled my back to his front.

"What the fuck was that?"

"I don't know. But I do know if Knox can deal with her being a loner, there may be hope for them."

I sure as heck hoped so. Fiona deserved some good in her life.

Chapter 11

'Boom, Bitch.'

Cotton

"Well, well, what do we have here?" Sanchez started out sitting in a leather booth at the only neutral bar in two states. Sadly, with it being December, the roads out here were getting less and less traversed. If this hadn't been an important meet, we wouldn't have come.

Snow had started falling on our way up here. Novalie just might be getting the white Christmas she had been dreaming about.

"Been years, Sanchez." It had been close to nearly seventeen years since we'd really sat down.

"Been years for what?" Sanchez knew what was about to come out of my mouth.

"Years since you said you owe me a marker."

The pale look that crossed his face said that Sanchez hoped I'd forgotten about all that. You don't ever forget when someone says that they owe you a marker.

"Fuck. Much as I hate you, I owe you. What is it?" The resigned look that came across Sanchez's face was probably the highlight of my whole god damn life, well maybe I shouldn't take it that far—that statement would have to be reserved for Novalie a thousand times over.

All the men's eyes that Sanchez had brought with him had closed. Yeah, fuckers. Y'all better get ready.

"Need you to tell me about Amy and French."

"That's it? I tell you about them and that's the marker?" A look of uncertainty was clear in his eyes. Of all the things that I could possibly ask of him, this was probably the most tame marker Sanchez had probably ever heard of. Hell, it was even the most tame that I had ever heard of.

But this was important to the club because Novalie had become our queen. It didn't matter if I hadn't publicly claimed her or not . . . yet. When my brothers asked her a question regarding the clubhouse, even if her word contradicted mine, here lately they had been following her directions. Normally, that would piss me the hell off, but nine times out of ten, she had been correct regardless.

"Yep." All that I could ask of Sanchez, our club's only real enemy, The Spades MC, and their president owed me a marker.

A marker that was given to me on the day that I'd taken a bullet for the man before we had become sworn enemies, when we were both only seventeen years old and Sanchez and his family moved to Tennessee. After that move, whatever had happened to the man that I once knew, had changed him irrevocably.

It took a minute before Sanchez started and the filth that he unloaded on us about Amy and French, fuck, I wanted to murder the both of them.

"To start, we didn't know French was one of yours. He prospected for us. Found his Wrath MC kutte when we suspected he was stealing from the club. It was in his duffle. The fucker told us he would make it even, and he gave us Amy and Novalie." Only I had expected a smug expression to be on his face, but that wasn't the look I'd caught a glimpse of. No, it was the look of sorrow.

Sorrow because Sanchez knew what Novalie had meant to me. Only that glimpse lasted a brief second and then he began to open his putrid mouth once more.

Before I could get up and rain terror on the place because my emotions were getting the best of me, the son of a bitch thought he could do that to Novalie. To my Kitten?

"That was why we were in your territory to begin with. We were coming to get ours. But your actions that night showed us that Novalie wasn't French's to give—she's yours. We don't break that rule. Ole' ladies are protected unless their man gives them over. But guess you got a right to know. French's body was dumped in a lake. Tried to steal from us again. Amy is now one of my men's ole' ladies."

"I'll tell the club about French, I doubt there will be any blowback seeing as he was banished from the club. Feel sorry for the fucker with Amy though." And with that, we walked out. Now, I just had to find a way to get ahold of Amy without starting a club war and making sure that my Kitten would be safe and taken care of.

What I hadn't expected was to be having a heart-to-heart with Novalie when I'd gotten home. It had been after we had eaten her world-famous lasagna and we were lying in bed.

"Kane, we've never talked about your mom and dad. I know you share things about your life with me when you're ready, but I'd like to know."

"Cancer. Cancer took my mom when I was five. My dad drank himself into oblivion a year later. Alcohol poisoning. My grandfather took me in. The day I turned eighteen, he signed all this over to me, and a week later, I walked into his house because I hadn't heard from him. Turned out he was battling stomach cancer and he fought until he knew I would be good. I owe him my life." And that was the truth.

"Then I guess we're a lot alike." She was the one person that if she told me that she knew how I felt, she did.

I fucking hated any time someone said they know how you feel. There was no way that you knew how someone really feels about anything. No two situations are the same, they may be considerably alike, but they are never the same.

"Yeah, babe, we are."

"I would've liked to have met him."

"Yeah, and I wouldn't have been able to handle it. He would've been hitting on you left and fucking right." And the look of doubt crossed her face, like it always did anytime I mentioned her looks. Her beauty was so fucking understated, it was crazy.

"Where are they buried?" For the life of me, I didn't know why she had asked me that until it was the next morning.

The next morning, Novalie forced me to take her to the flower shop where she assaulted me with what my mother's favorite color was if I could even remember it, but strangely enough I did.

How did she force me? She told me no more blow jobs. I would roll over and whine like a newborn pup to get those from her.

Her mouth was like a work of art.

And so, after she picked out lavender irises, we drove to the cemetery where my parents and my grandfather had been buried on his bike.

Yes, that had been my grandfather's last wish. He had already paid the cemetery to have it done for him. It also helped that he had been friends with the owner.

All with Novalie keeping the flowers safe in the zip-up hoodie that she was wearing.

"Kane, give me a few moments alone with her. Please?" And whether she really knew it or not, she didn't even have to say please. I would do whatever she asked of me as long as it was within my power to do so.

"Yeah, babe."

I watched as she walked over to my father's grave first as she placed one flower atop his plot, then she did the same with my grandfather's but she placed a kiss to two fingers then she placed her hand atop his head stone, that woman owned every inch of me. Then she went over to my mother's.

When she knelt down, unknowingly to me, I'd edged forward to hear what she had to say, when I heard the words, it felt as though I had been intruding into their moment.

"Thank you for making that amazing man. Thank you for instilling in him to protect, to care, and to love. I love your son, so very much. I hope that through my actions, I may be somewhat worthy of your approval . . ."

Then I felt the pull. My body was pulled away by an unknowing force, I stood there in awe of the woman who had quickly brightened my dark heart and filled it up with so much purity, it was unreal.

Fuck, but I loved that woman with everything in me. Now, the next step was to put my baby in her and solidify her place that was neither in front of me, nor behind me, but beside me, where she will forever stay.

When she had walked back over to me, I offered her my rough, calloused hand so she could place hers in my protective embrace, "I love you, beautiful," I said after I placed a kiss on her temple.

That night, after she cooked some mean chicken, she had headed out to the deck with that shoebox in her hands. I had been on a call with York regarding a charity run we were planning.

The charity run was for the local school system to get them new computers.

When I ended the call, I made my way out to her.

"Kitten, want to tell me what's in the shoebox?" That shoebox had always been in the back of my mind. Her clothes had all seemed to have been torn and mended over the years and they had no doubt seen better days. All of this made me want to find that poor excuse of a mother she has and beat the ever-loving shit out of her. I didn't hit women, but damn, my patience was gone. However, that shoebox appeared to be in excellent condition, like it had been her most sacred treasure.

"It's my baby stuff. I found it in the garbage bin when I was six. Apparently, my good old mother didn't want any more remembrance that she had once carried me." God damn, I wanted to find that bitch and teach her all about respect and family, and just fuck. I roared out in my mind as to not scare her.

I just didn't understand how people could be so careless when it came to children. It wasn't their fault that they were born into this world. If you didn't think that you can be the parent that they need and if you can't shower them with unconditional love, then give them to someone that will pour every ounce of their soul into that baby.

"Kitten, I'm sorry, babe." I didn't apologize to anyone for anything, but for her, I would walk on my knees every day of my life if that was what she would ask of me.

"I don't know if it's in the cards for us or not, but what I do know is that I never want my children to feel any less important than that they are our whole world."

"I'm with you Kitten. Never really wanted kids until you." And I didn't. I didn't want to bring a child into this world with anyone who I didn't deem as perfect in my eyes. But that's really a lie. God makes everyone perfect in his eyes, it's just up to us to find our own kind of perfect.

That was Novalie.

It was at that moment that she left her chair and climbed into my lap. She pulled out the little things and showed me, even told me that if it was in the cards for us, then she wanted to hand some of her own stuff down to them.

As the crickets sang, we sat there in the quiet of night. As we were looking up at the stars, she smiled every time she spotted a constellation up in the night sky.

My Kitten fell asleep shortly after we had talked, as always, her light, soft snore sent fire straight to my dick. Even her snores turned me the fuck on.

Chapter 12

'Karma is a Bitch.'

Novalie

I was about to clock out and head home after pulling a double because Virginia was training the replacement for Deidra when my phone rang, it was Lucy.

"Hey, Luce." I was tired and hoped that nothing major had happened in the club. I wanted to go home and soak my aching feet.

Here lately, it seemed anytime anything went down, I got a phone call as well as Cotton.

"Hey, Novalie." Yeah, by the tone that came across the speaker, there was a problem.

"What's up?" Here we go again. Time to bust a bitch's face up. Only what I thought was going to come across the speaker was far from reality.

"There's a man here looking for you. He's in a suit." A suit? "Cop?" I hoped not. It wasn't that Cotton had told me a lot, but he didn't lie to me any time I asked about something that had to do with the club. I just watched how certain situations made him feel.

Unfortunately, since we weren't married, they could come after me due to there not being a spousal privilege involved. Albeit I also knew that Cotton wouldn't let anyone bring harm to me. Nor would I ever betray the trust that Cotton has given me.

"Nope, a lawyer."

"Okay, I'll be right there." Why in the world was a lawyer at the clubhouse looking for me?

After we hung up, I called Cotton. And like clockwork, he picked up on the second ring.

"Yeah, Kitten?" Still, after all these months, his voice sent shudders down my spine.

"Where are you?" I had known from experience that normally the members wouldn't answer that question, but with Cotton, he would.

"On the way back from making a run. Be back in thirty." I could hear the wind ripping by him. He had his earbuds in his ears.

When I had needed to get ahold of him one time on his birthday, he had forgotten them. He never left home without them again.

"Okay. Lucy called and said there was a man in a suit at the clubhouse looking for me. I asked her if he was a cop and she said he was a lawyer," I rushed that out. I didn't like taking his attention away from the road.

Too many times when I had been on the back of his bike, people seriously didn't pay attention to bikes. They really needed to start doing so.

"Be there in twenty, Kitten. Wait for me to talk to him." Yeah, he was more than likely going to be there in fifteen minutes.

"Okay, Kane," I murmured out.

"Love you, Kitten." At those words, I melted all over again the same way I did the first time he said he loved me back.

"Love you too, Kane."

On the drive to the clubhouse, I ran through scenarios for why some lawyer would be coming to see me. And why would that lawyer know to come to the clubhouse?

In about ten minutes, I made it to the clubhouse. And there in the driveway was a black Lincoln Continental.

When I parked the truck in Cotton's spot, which was really my spot now, I climbed out.

I got a chin lift from Walker who had been on Novalie detail today. He was letting me know that he was here if I needed to go anywhere and that he was still on duty while I was inside those walls without Cotton.

I noticed the door to the car open and out came the man in the suit. He was an older man with white hair with hazel eyes. Not as tall as Cotton, but he wasn't a slouch either.

"Miss Novalie Henderson?"

"If you don't mind waiting a few minutes, I'm waiting for someone to get here." I'd never talked with a lawyer before either.

"That is perfectly fine. Would it be possible to go inside and get a cold drink?" I noticed him fanning himself. While it wasn't a hot one today, it was the humidity that made the day a scorcher.

"Of course." I smiled and led the way into the clubhouse.

When we entered, I turned to him, "What would you like?"

"A cold soda would be great."

"What can I get for you, Novalie?" It was Vas who asked. We had come to an understanding the night she tried to get in my face at the barbeque.

"Two cold sodas, Vas. Thanks." I was glad that I now called her a close friend. I didn't know if any of the brothers were going to make her an ole' lady, but I did know that she had turned her sights completely away from Cotton and she was now looking at the club's Enforcer, Garret.

"You got it." Vas smiled.

"I've never been inside a clubhouse," the man said.

"Yeah, this place is my second home. A safe place." There was no other place that I felt so safe in. Our house, Cotton's arms, and this brick building.

"It's not what I expected. I expected naked girls and booze, drugs, men with beer bellies and the like. Not to mention the long greasy hair from being on the road and untamed beards."

I laughed at that thought as Vas came over with our drinks. "Thanks again, Vas." I smiled.

"Well, you are more than welcome to come here at nighttime. This whole place changes." It was never this quiet at night, not with all of the brothers ending the night off with booze, girls, and loud music. It was perfect.

"I can believe that. Oh, before I forget, my name is Eric Connors," he stated as he also slipped out a business card from a place in his wallet.

"Pleased to meet you." I smiled at him and then the front door opened and in walked Cotton with five brothers right behind him.

I saw him scan the room, when his eyes landed on mine, he came over.

"You okay, Kitten?" he asked me as he placed his thumb and forefinger under my chin, assessing if all was okay without my saying so.

"Yeah, Kane." He glanced at the other man and then brought another chair over to our table and sat down. But not before he kissed my forehead. It was simply Cotton. He got as close to me with our thighs touching. As soon as our bodies touched, it felt like our clothes had caught on fire.

"As I was telling Novalie, my name is Eric Connors. I'm a lawyer." Normally, anytime anyone came to the clubhouse in a suit, it meant that shit was about to hit the fan, literally.

"Cotton," he offered him his hand.

"I thought she just called you . . ." The confusion was evident on the lawyer's face.

"She's the only one who calls me Kane. Her and her alone. To everyone else, I'm Cotton." Cotton hadn't really had to state that to a lot of people. Anyone in the MC knew those words for what they were.

"Okay, my mistake." It was then that he got the gravity of the situation but barely.

"Now, the reason that I'm here is to sadly inform you, Miss Henderson, that your grandfather, Henry Henderson, passed away three months ago. It has taken me this long to find you. Had we not hired a private investigator to find you after your mother continued to lie to us, I never would have found you."

"Wait, my mother told me that I didn't have any grandparents." Anytime I had tried to push Amy for any information on my family, I got shut down.

"I'm not surprised, Novalie. To be honest, I don't think much of your mother." Well, at least he was being honest, and he was correct in his assumption.

"You ain't alone in that," came from Cotton. As well as multiple words of agreement from the brothers who now surrounded our table.

Almost as if they were prepared to throw themselves in front of me if the need arose for them to do so.

"So, my grandfather," I said, wanting to get this over with. I felt bad about it all, but since I had never met the man, how was I to grieve in that sense?

"Yes, your grandfather . . ." And it was then that the lawyer's mask of indifference showed through. "Umm, he . . . uh . . . well, he had a will." Sweat beads could be seen in the crease of his forehead. It was then that I got why he was suddenly nervous.

"Mr. Connors, if you're true and you don't try to mess with me, none of these men will lay a hand on you." I knew why he had started to act as if they were about to jump on him. They could be intimidating just by standing there, not to mention these men presented a horrifying front.

"Well, umm okay then. Now, like I said, your grandfather had a will. I have that will with me. Now, is there somewhere that we can speak privately?"

"Mr. Connors, I see where your mind is going, and under a different circumstance, we could talk privately, but sir, I trust these men with my life. Whatever is in there, they can hear."

"Ms. Henderson . . ." No, that was my mother.

"It's Novalie." I wouldn't be called Henderson any longer.

"Right, Novalie, considering the contents in this will, I really think it would behoove you to hear this in private."

"Mr. Connors, I'll either not hear the will at all, or you can reveal the information in front of me now. I really hate having to repeat myself." I would never speak like that to anyone, but I really didn't appreciate the man judging the men behind me without knowing them.

This I would not be swayed in. Cotton had shown me the meaning of trust time and time again. With this man, even if the whole world were to ever turn on me, he would be right there. Not to mention the men in this MC. They were as good as gold.

"Okay, Ms. Hen—Novalie. This is the last will and living testament of Henry Henderson, your grandfather."

And when he read the very last word, my whole body was in shock.

"You mean to tell me that bitch fucking knew about Novalie's grandfather wanting custody of her? She knew about the money that was rightfully to go to Novalie? You mean to tell me, that she has been on her own since she was twelve god damn years old, and she could have been given the world then?" The lawyer visibly shrank in his seat at Cotton's words/

It was something else to see Cotton pissed off. Even the tick in his jaw was in overdrive.

"York, place a call to Sanchez. Get word that we want to have a little old meet with Amy." I could tell that the waiting game on finding her mother had just been amped up to the highest priority.

"York, it's okay. I've got a way to get a hold of her." Had I still been looking at York, I would have seen the nod. He answered to Cotton and to me. And all of the brothers also just saw that as well.

"I also have a letter for you. I'll read it aloud for you." I watched in earnest, curious as to the contents as he opened the envelope.

"Dear Novalie, I doubt your mom ever told you, but your father fought tooth and nail to get you. Unfortunately, cancer didn't let him finish the battle, so he had to step back. It was then that I had tried to be granted custody, however with my aging and my own medical problems, the courts wouldn't hear of it. I truly am sorry. It was then that your father was told that you had been placed for adoption. He found this out after he beat the cancer. He has been in remission ever since. With no leads on which way to go about finding you, he had to give up. I do hope this letter finds you in good company. All my love, princess. Love, your grandfather. Oh, and P.S. Look for a man named Preacher. That's your father."

I couldn't help myself as I got out of my chair and crawled into Cotton's lap. I cried for all that I had missed. All that had been taken from me. All because of my selfish mother. I knew that it is wrong to hate someone, but I hated my mother.

"Preacher? You mean that old man who lives up in the cabin out of town?" York had asked the room.

"Wait, you know him?" I asked York while tears were still running out of the corners of my eyes.

"Well, yeah, Kitten. We make runs up there to check on him. Never did I think he was your father or I would have told you," Cotton whispered in my hair.

"I see what you mean about these men, Novalie," the lawyer stated and the sweat was gone from his forehead.

I didn't know what caused my reaction, but it was a coming to the lights moment for the lawyer that I busted out laughing, the tears then turned into joy.

"What do you mean?" I asked him between bouts of laughter.

"None of them even flinched when I mentioned how much money you inherited and the property. The only thing they flinched about was the treatment your mother did to you and the fact that your father is still alive."

"They're the best." They were absolutely the best of men.

And the men all had smiles at my back that I judged from the small number of chuckles I had received.

"Now, can you get word to my mother and tell her that I'm denying the money and that it goes to her?" The only person who hadn't tried to sway me had been Cotton. He knew.

"What?" The lawyer wore an exasperating but shocked look upon his face.

"Novalie, why would you ask him to—" York stopped short as I threw my hand up and explained my reasoning.

"Tell her that. But have her meet you at Virginia's Diner in town. Once she sits down, you apologize and move away. I'll slide into the booth and have a little chat with her."

It was then that Cotton pulled out his phone and placed a call.

"Virginia, yeah, going to be something going down at your diner . . ." Cotton sat quiet for a moment. "Yeah, it's for Novalie, finally getting to have words with her bitch of a mother."

"Right. Yeah? Okay, thanks." Cotton shut his phone off.

It shouldn't have surprised me that it had only taken the lawyer to get a response from my mother within the hour.

The very next day, it was myself along with Cotton, York, Garret, and Cooper, who all stood in the back room with eyes on the booth that the lawyer was sitting in.

And then I saw my mother. And in that instant, I was damn right grateful that I hadn't gotten my looks from my mother. I had guessed it was all due to my father. As strange as it was to be said, my mother looked even worse now than the last time I had seen her.

She was strung out on something heavy, that was for sure. And then I saw her new man and my heart dropped. I didn't know it, but I had tightened my hand that was held in Cotton's grasp.

"What is it, Kitten?"

"That man with my mom. He was in the house one night, crept into my room. I was nine then. He came closer to my bed and was unzipping his pants when something was knocked against the window and he stopped cold. Something about what he saw when he looked out the window had him zipping up his pants and leaving my room. I got up and put a chair under my door, but when I looked out the window, I didn't see anything. It happened once more when I turned fourteen. But again, something knocked against my window and the man left my room." That started me thinking.

"I'll fucking kill him." Yeah, I maybe shouldn't have told Cotton all of that.

"So, I'm here. What do I need to do?" Even Amy's voice carried her appearance. For a small instant I almost felt sorry for her. Almost being the key word here.

"You do understand that your daughter refused this money and that's why you are able to receive it, correct?"

"I don't give a fuck what that little bitch says that money is rightfully mine. He was my father, not hers." I wanted to know what it was that I had ever done to her.

"Then I'll go grab the forms from my car. I'll return in just a moment." And then, it was almost time.

"First thing I'm going to do is hire a professional and kill that little tramp . . ." Before she said another word, Cotton was no longer at my side, but he had his hand wrapped around my mother's neck.

"Novalie says the word, I'll personally put you out of your misery. And I'll love every fucking single second of it." And while he was making that promise, Garret had pulled his piece from a nearby booth where he sat on the man who had come with my mother.

But before anything else had been done, and while Cotton still had Amy's neck in his hand, he pulled his piece and pointed it at the other man as well.

"You ever step foot in my town again, I'll blow your goddamn brains out. I ought to kill you for the shit you tried to pull on Novalie, but I will not dirty up this diner. Now, you have five seconds to get the fuck out of my sight before I revoke my promise to Virginia and splatter your brains all over these walls."

"Hank, where do you think—" Amy started to say but was wisely told to shut the fuck up.

"You're on your own with this shit, Amy. You were never my ole' lady, I just wanted all that damn money. But have to say, babe, either learn to keep those damn legs closed or tighten that shit up. Fucking sloppy is the name of your pussy." Then the man named Hank split.

So, it was then that I slid into the other side of the booth and faced my mother as I nodded at my man to let her go.

However, I refused to call her that any longer. Just because she gave birth to me, that didn't mean that she had earned that right.

"Amy, nice to see you."

"You think you're so above me now? Darlin', you ain't jack fucking shit." Just the sight of her was making me sick.

"No, but I'm a better person than you." And I knew that I was.

"Yeah, you thought you always had been. Why do you think I tried to get that pansy to end your life once I learned what my precious father had planned?" This vile creature did not deserve my tears and I refused to allow her another minute of my time.

I snarled out, and I despised curse words coming out of my mouth, but in this instant, I deserved it. "Because you're a sick fucking human being."

"You're no better than me. You were spreading your legs for any man who would show you an ounce of emotion. You and your daddy issues," Amy said as she looked over at Cotton seductively.

I refused to react to that. Amy didn't deserve it.

"Wrong. I was a virgin until Cotton took me in and actually showed me what love really was." I knew that he wouldn't get upset with me for calling him Cotton at this moment. The bitch didn't have the right to know anything about us.

"So, you spread for the mighty big Cotton? He's nothing but scum of the earth and—" That was when I lost any ounce of respect that I may have had for her, I reached across the tabletop and backhanded Amy's cheek.

"I don't give a damn what you say about me. But you think for one second that I will sit here and allow you to say something about Cotton, you deceitful uncaring bitch? Then you have another thing coming."

"Well, well, well, you've finally grown some balls, I see." *Real classy*, I thought.

"No, but I do have a great pussy that my man fucking loves. What do you have? Something dried out and used up? Oh wait, one that's sloppy, right?" I heard the smirks from all of the men, but I didn't bother to look at them. Not when I wanted this done so that I didn't have to deal with Amy not one more minute longer.

"She does that," I heard the smile in his voice as Cotton murmured.

Which in turn caused me to have to fight my own smile.

"So, tell me, Amy, why do you hate me so much?" That was the million-dollar question, one that I always wanted answered but highly doubted I would ever get a straight answer unfortunately.

But it would seem that something had Amy taking the truth serum today.

"Because you took my life from me. My body went to hell after I popped your sorry ass out."

"That's called being a mom, which you haven't been much of one."

"Oh, really? I've taken care of you your whole damn life."

"Bullshit. The last time you did anything for me was when I was twelve and that was the last time you cared enough about me to pay the damn electric bill. It's been me ever since. Where were you when I broke my arm? Where were you when I had the flu? Hell, where were you when the man came into my room when I was six, unzipping his pants. You're nothing but a used-up cunt. You've never been my mother."

"Well, guess it's a good thing that you're rid of me after I sign those papers." Amy looked smug.

And here we go. "See, funny thing about that is, I'm not denying the money. I signed the necessary paperwork yesterday." I relished in the look that came across Amy's face.

The look of fear and hatred that flashed across her face when the new reality hit her. Freaking priceless.

"You little bitch—" Before she could get another word out of her mouth, it wasn't Cotton who stepped in. No, it was a man I have never seen before but who I swore looked familiar. He came to our table and placed his hands on either side of Amy.

And then it hit me—I have looked at that same face every single time I looked in the mirror.

"You are the scum of the fucking earth, you backstabbing, gold-digging whore. You fucking left her alone when she broke her arm? Had I known what all was really going down, I could've taken my daughter from you, you goddamn piece of shit. Prison sentence be damned. How dare you tell me that you gave my daughter up for adoption? You had no goddamn right. But you know what? That's okay. Because I've got a little surprise for you."

Then he turned to me.

"It's like I'm looking in a mirror. You're beautiful, Novalie. You look a lot like your grandmother. After I get through taking care of this, me and you are going to have a relationship. I hope that's okay with you."

"Yes, that would be perfect." And it really would be perfect. Perhaps I would at least have a member of my family who actually gave a damn. "Can I ask you a question?"

"Of course, sweetheart." I hadn't been the only one who had noticed the difference in his tone when he had spoken to me and not to Amy.

"When did you learn that she didn't give me up for adoption?"

"The day you turned six, I saw you running and laughing with your friend, June. I followed you there. I sat outside most nights. I didn't like the sort of men who came in and out of your house. I also know you're going to ask why I didn't step in and get you out of there. I was sick for a long-time, sweetheart. I'm sure your grandfather explained a great deal. But really, all I can say about any of it, is that I'll be in your life from here on out and I'll bust my ass to be the father that you deserve, and maybe one day you'll call me dad." He smiled. Yeah, I definitely took more from him than I did Amy.

When I nodded, he turned to Cotton. "Good. Cotton, okay with you if I escort this whore out of here?"

"Yeah, man. So long as she leaves Novalie the fuck alone, I don't give a god damn. She goes away that'll be the best for everyone involved."

And that was that. My father then hauled Amy out of the diner.

"Well, that went well." As ever, York was the mood killer.

"Let's head to the clubhouse. I feel the need to let loose a little. That felt great." I was going to talk Cotton into letting me have a drink. After all of that, I deserved it. Besides, since when did bikers really follow the law after all?

With my hand wrapped tightly in Cotton's, we all left the diner.

We rode in a procession with Cotton and me taking the lead while York and Cooper were behind us, and then back behind them were Garret and Xavier taking up the rear.

As soon as we rode into the yard, rounds of cheers went up. It was all for me. Somehow, they had already gotten a call because the grills were turned on, drinks were being poured, and music started thumping all over the confines on the compound of Wrath MC.

That night, instead of going home, we had crawled into Cotton's bed at the clubhouse around three a.m. and we didn't come up for air until eleven that next morning.

Alcohol breath didn't taste that well in the morning.

"Do we have any snack cakes or anything?" I asked aloud in the kitchen. I was craving something sweet.

"Well, Cotton does have a shelf that's just for him, and I figure you're the only one that he would allow access to that," Vas said from her position at the stove top.

So, me being myself, as well as his Kitten, I opened the pantry and went straight to his shelf. Well, hot damn, my man had been holding out on me. I should have known better. I knew that he considered five places sacred to himself and I had been wondering where the fifth place was. Well, he did have them to himself before we got together, but he never mentioned this particular shelf. That man.

When Cotton entered into the kitchen for lunch, I had a Little Debbie's box sitting in front of me and I was snacking down.

"Fucking really? Can I not have one goddamn thing to myself?" he roared out as I took another bite.

"Do you want a blow job tonight?" Of course, that would definitely get the reaction that I wanted, and a minute later, it did.

The all-knowing look I caught on his face before he dipped his head down said it all.

"You're going to be the death of me." He smiled, making those dimples of his pop out.

"But what a way to go, baby." Then I tore into another cake. "I love you, Kane," I murmured around yet another bite of that chocolatey goodness.

"After I get my blowjob, I'm eating you out and you're not shoving me away when you've had enough. I'll decide when you've had enough." He gave me a kiss and out the door he went.

Totally not caring who was around.

With a response like that, I just freaking smiled . . . a megawatt smile.

"Girl!" All the ladies squealed.

That afternoon, when all the brothers had piled out of church, the women stood off to the side as Justin handed Lucy his kutte for her to sew on his patches. They had patched him in as a brother.

"You better remember what I told you. The first moment you disrespect Novalie, you're fucking out. I don't give a damn that you're a brother," Cotton said as he slapped Justin on the back of his shoulder.

After dinner was made and served to the brothers, I saw a usually upbeat York sitting at one of the picnic benches with his head in his hands.

Not liking that one bit, I walked over to him.

"Hey, York."

"Hey, darlin'." Even if he was in a bad mood, he never failed to acknowledge me with ' 'darlin''.

"I'm here if you want to talk," I said to him. I knew all too well that if you pushed someone and they weren't ready to reveal any information, it would just make them close up all the more.

So, I just sat there with him, not saying a word, silently letting him know that I wouldn't push.

It wasn't until Cotton called my name that I got up to leave York's side, but then he suddenly grabbed a hold of my wrist.

"Ever feel like something is staring you in the face, but you just don't know what it is yet?"

"Sometimes. Then I remember everything happens for a reason and we just have to be patient."

"Not sure if what is going on really requires patience," he muttered.

"Do you think that whatever it is wouldn't be worth the wait?"

"I don't know, darlin', honestly. You know a lot of shit is still hazy and I still don't remember anything before I woke up in that hospital bed. But this, something just feels right."

"I get that. But whatever it is, whenever it presents itself, just do you and follow whatever feels right. And it will be perfect."

"Thanks, darlin', for a young one, you sure do know a lot."

As I walked away from the table my chest felt heavy for York. I just wished I knew what all was really going on.

"Everything okay, Kitten?"

"Yeah, something is going on with York."

"I noticed that too. I can't really explain a whole lot because to be honest I don't know the whole of it myself. What I do know is that something from his past meant a great deal to him, and now he can't have it. But I have a feeling that things are about to hit the fan with him."

Crazy how life can change in the blink of an eye.

Chapter 13

'Best present ever.'

Cotton

It was Christmas Eve and I had been pleased to see that my Kitten had yet to get me anything because we'd made a deal.

Soon as I walked through the door after making sure the clubhouse was ready for our Christmas dinner, I knew I shouldn't have expected her to not get me anything.

"Thought we agreed on no presents, Kitten," I said to her as she was putting the finishing touches on a present in the middle of the living room floor.

"Yeah, I know, but I promise you a blowjob if you don't love everything that's under our tree."

"Then I'll make sure I show my displeasure," I told her as I had to bite my bottom lip to hide the smile.

We were curled up on our couch watching one of her favorite movies, she spoke right along with the movie when the man said, 'Why would you want to marry me for, anyhow'.

And it was at that moment when Novalie climbed atop me and said, 'So I can kiss you anytime I want'. Then she planted that perfect mouth on mine.

With that, I was so close to placing the ring that was burning a hole in the pocket of my kutte on her finger.

But I had to wait. I had something planned that had to take place first and that meant more in the MC world than anywhere else on the planet. Even to myself.

The next morning, I was so damn happy that she got over that fucking morning breath shit when she rolled over.

"Merry Christmas, Kane." She rolled over and kissed my bearded cheek.

"Merry Christmas, Kitten," I murmured out. It was our first and our first of many.

"I love you, Kane." Those words right there, if she only ever spoke those words to me for the rest of our lives, I would die a happy man.

"Love you too, Kitten."

And with that, I rolled over, climbed atop the woman then had my breakfast underneath our covers.

"Always perfect, Kitten," I said after I ate my breakfast.

Afterwards, her moaning while she had been soaping up in the shower had the effect of making me rock hard, so I couldn't let a perfect opportunity go to waste. We made love in the shower. That shower was now one of my favorite places of all.

But my favorite place was in the garage. Because just last week, she surprised me by having her ass in the air over the seat of my bike. Something about making love on your bike with your woman. It had definitely been one for the books.

Since she finished her shower before I did, when she stepped out, she turned to me. "I'll have your clothes laid out for you on the bed. This is for me. And I'm asking please."

Curious to what the hell she had done now, I hurried through the rest of my shower.

And when I opened the bathroom door, there on the bed was a pair of plaid flannel pajama pants and a black tee, I smiled.

My fucking woman. Just for her would I put myself through this shit.

And it was worth the shit when I walked into the living room and saw her with two coffee mugs, wearing the same outfit as myself and her camera at the ready.

So yes, I did my job and made my Kitten happy. We took a few photos and she declared one of them for the mantle. What I didn't know was that she also posted almost all of them to social media.

And when I saw the photos after she had shoved the camera in my face, I noticed the two coffee mugs, one of them said 'Mommy' and one said 'Daddy'.

It was then that I gave her a look and said, "What the fuck?" Then she smiled and handed me a gift box.

So unsure was I since she was always playing a prank or something, I slightly shrugged the mugs off.

"I told you I didn't want anything, Kitten."

"Well, suck it up, Kane, and get over it. When you said you loved me back, this is what you get."

"I'm damn fucked," I said, smiling at her, she pinched my side all the while laughing.

"Little shit." And it was with her that I had laughed more in the past seven months than I had my whole life.

When she leaned in and kissed my cheek, she whispered, "Love you, Kane."

So, I unwrapped my gift.

And inside were two pairs of motorcycle boots. One pink pair and one blue pair. My heart started to race. Below the boots was a folded-up paper with the words 'Will I be a He or a She'?

When I opened the paper with my heart in my throat, settled neatly was a picture. An ultrasound. And on that ultrasound, was a little blob.

"The fuck am I looking at? It's so damn blurry, I can't see a damn thing." And just my luck that I couldn't see a damn thing when I knew it was important.

"Sweetheart, we're only seven weeks. It'll grow every day." She wore an unsure expression on her face, if I wasn't feeling giddy that one of my dreams may have just came true, I'd haul her into my lap and kiss the fuck out of her mouth until she was so sure about herself.

"You mean what I think you mean?" Was she telling me we were going to have a baby for real?

"My baby inside you?" I felt the tears at the corners of my eyes. My dream.

"Yes, Kane." This woman, this masterpiece that God built just for me.

It was at that moment that my whole entire world just came full circle. So, I bent low and pressed my lips to her belly.

"Hey there, little ass-kicker. Mommy and Daddy can't wait to meet. We love you."

Then I grabbed her and hauled her body to mine and made love to her ever so carefully on the floor in front of our first Christmas tree, the blazing fire roaring in the fireplace while Christmas carols played.

Even though I told her I would be displeased with what was under that tree, there was no way in hell I would ever be disappointed with what she had given me.

And yes, you guessed it, she still gave me that blowjob and though she was still learning about what pleased me, I came even faster when she had reached her hand down her underwear and pleased herself in the process.

"Kitten, let's fucking go already." We were supposed to be at the club like half an hour ago.

"I'm coming, keep your pantyhose on."

"You better not be putting on that fucking war paint. I don't know why the fuck you insist on wearing it," I grumbled. Damn shit was nothing but trash. Her skin looked perfect without it.

"Kane, quit your shit. Do I ever bitch about you being late for dinner? Do I ever bitch about you having to leave me at a restaurant to go handle club shit? No. So don't you dare bitch at me for putting on a little makeup that makes me feel good about myself," she chastised me.

"Well, just get a move on, would you?" Then I heard it in her voice. She was smiling at me because she knew she just won that show down. Yet again.

"Of course, sweetheart." Her sing-song voice carried through the house.

When she emerged from our bathroom ten minutes later, I decided that she could take however long she needed in the bathroom to get ready.

But we were seriously late and technically that was my fault, but I pinned it on her. Had she not walked out of the bathroom dressed like she was, then I never would have wrapped my hands around her ass and hauled her up my body and slammed her against the wall, then made her scream my name. Loud enough that the people in the clubhouse probably heard.

An hour later, when we finally made it to the clubhouse, we were all gathered in the main room. I whistled for York to grab everyone's attention, then I nodded at my Kitten to come over to me.

I subtly nodded to Lucy as well.

"First of all, I wanted to thank each and every one of you for being here and being a part of this MC but also this family. We have new blood in our club and new prospects. We have additions to the family. And one of them, well, two of them, we're making official today. Lucy, can you bring it here please?"

Everyone watched and carved a path for Lucy as she carried a kutte over to us.

"Thanks, Lucy," I said as I grabbed the leather kutte from her hands and smiled when Lucy kissed Novalie's cheek.

I would more than likely have a bawling-over emotional woman in my arms tonight, truth be told, I couldn't fucking wait.

"Today, we further welcome into the fold the woman who holds us all together and the woman who holds every piece of me in the palm of her hands. Here's to my ole' lady, Novalie."

Grinning, I held the property kutte up so Novalie could slip her arms in it.

Rounds of whoops and congratulations came from all around the room.

"Thought you said two of them we were making official?" Garret murmured off to the right of the group. Smart as fucking ever, that one.

And in an action that needed no words, as was my way, I pulled Novalie in front of me and quickly slipped the princess cut diamond ring onto her fourth finger on her left hand then splayed my hands on her belly and just fucking smiled.

"Wait?" Garret sounded, looking confused.

"Why you smiling like—" Cooper popped off.

"You're going to have a baby?" Cree squealed from beside her dad.

"She's carrying my baby!" I roared out at the crowd.

"Second generation of Cotton badassery. Fuck yeah!" York cheered.

Words of congratulations and warm greetings with well-wishes came from the forty-something person group. If I knew anything our baby was going to be spoiled ass fucking rotten.

Then it happened a lot sooner than I expected, a whimpering Novalie turned in my arms and buried her face in my neck. I dipped low, picked her up in my arms, and strode over to the back table.

Warm trails were tearing their way down his neck.

"Kitten, are you okay?" It took everything in me to not laugh, seeing as that was all I ever did when she got into one of these moods.

Especially when she finally noticed the weight from the rock on her finger, her megawatt smile was bright as tears again filled her eyes.

"Yeah, I've just never been this happy in my whole life and I get to be the lucky as heck woman who gets to call herself Mrs. Novalie Ann O'Malley." It was then that I threw my head back and roared with laughter.

Yes, I did good. My woman was fucking happy, I had made it official to all that I treasured her above all else. She was and would forever be my world.

I thanked my lucky stars that out of all the men in the world, she had chosen me to love. After a life that had been filled with nothing but endless fucks and emotional disconnect from anyone who wasn't club, I was finally whole. She was my savior.

Epilogue

Novalie

The day we had chosen for our wedding was perfect. The weather had been just right. It wasn't too hot and there was even a light breeze. It had been exactly one year to the date when Cotton had taken me from that house. Lucy, Vas, Fiona, and Cree helped me pick out my wedding dress. Sadly, June had been unavailable, and I had given up when I'd reached out to her and told her about the baby.

The first salon we had strolled into had been the one. Of course, it had been the sixth dress that I tried on, but it was my dress. And yes, I said yes to the dress.

It was a form-fitted mermaid silhouette with a sweetheart neckline, and it had a corset down the back. It had been everything that I had ever dreamed of and then some. My hair was plaited and even I loved that we had mimicked Elsa's style with my hair. Yes, I was nineteen years old, and too old for *Frozen*, but that was okay too. And because of the shade of my hair, they wove a piece of crimson lace through the braid. It was perfect.

However, one of my all-time favorite moments had been when the priest had announced, "Now, may I present to you, for the first time ever, Mr. And Mrs. Kane Michael O'Malley."

My father had made it a point to be in my life regardless of what it was. He had been there for every single event. He also walked me down the aisle to my forever.

We had gotten married underneath that willow tree. After the ceremony and the reception, Cotton carved our names into the trunk.

I had done what Cotton had asked and had chosen the school that I most desired, and luckily, because of my admission essay, they allowed me to attend virtually. I just had to do clinicals at a local hospital whenever that time came.

It was also that day that my father had pulled us aside and told us what really happened to Amy. She had gotten sick after she mysteriously got her hands on some rat poisoning. What a shame.

No one had even been looking for her. However, I had gotten wind a few days later that her death was officially ruled a suicide.

Four Years Later

I had been reminiscing about that perfect day as we were window shopping down the main drag in town.

It was also then that I recalled the first time ever, two years ago, when I was told to go into the house after grocery shopping by my little heartthrob because his daddy and him had the groceries. When his two-year-old self grabbed a bag and started to carry it, it pulled him down. But did that stop his progress? No, he fell forward three more times until I just couldn't take it any longer and scooped him up, bag and all. I kissed his little cheeks, which then resulted in his dimples popping out.

It was at that moment that I realized he wasn't quite my little boy anymore. Especially not when I heard his perfect little voice say, "Daddy, that boy drives a piece of shit."

Cotton

My four-year-old clone yelled out while we were walking on the sidewalk following a waddling Novalie. She had a craving for a warm peanut fudge brownie, and I knew she was tired of being cooped up in the house.

"Jasper, that's right. Only punk ass pussies drive any bike that's not a Harley." I shouldn't have said that.

"Right, Daddy. We ain't no punk ass pussies. We drive Harleys," my little man said from beside me. Fuck, I really shouldn't have said that. I was one in trouble daddy.

"Kane, he keeps speaking like that, you're not getting any!" Yeah, I definitely shouldn't have said that. And my wife didn't give a fuck who heard her any longer.

When we had first met, she never even cussed. Yes, she let her temper flare, but only when we were in private. And now, five years later, she didn't go easy on me.

"But Mommy, we only speaking the truth. Don't keep the cookies from Daddy." Damn, he was about to get his daddy into trouble.

We had started referring to making love by saying we couldn't wait to get some cookies from the cookie jar. So, any time we had that particular conversation where Novalie was threatening to withhold any from me, Jasper thought it was a cookie.

He was my whole world, well, besides Novalie, the club, and one other little thing.

"I never should have agreed to you getting his first project bike for his birthday," she mumbled as we were entering a bakery that her friend Sydney owned.

We had to come three towns over to satisfy her craving. The bakery in our town had the brownies, but she stated they were nowhere near as good as Sydney's.

As soon as we sat down with her brownie, a cookie for Jasper, and a black coffee for me, my wife looked at me when she had the brownie in her mouth, her eyes were as round as a fishbowl.

"You okay, Kitten?" I didn't like the look she was giving me.

She mumbled something around her brownie and then her face got pale. My heart started to pound in my chest.

"Kitten, what's wrong?" There was a look I hated seeing across her beautiful face.

"Daddy, why's the floor so wet?" Jasper had asked at my side, and when I looked down, it was then I saw the puddle of water and Novalie's wet dress.

"Your water broke?" I whispered-yelled.

"What?" came from Sydney as she rounded the counter in a hurry, pushing past customers as she made her way over to us.

As if it were second nature, I had my cell in my hand as I looked at Sydney.

"Be back with my truck," I told Sydney.

"Be right back, Kitten. Jasper, take care of your momma." I knelt down, kissed my wife's forehead, and out the door I went, all the while I was yelling in my phone at York, issuing out orders.

As soon as I made it back to the bakery, I carried Novalie to the truck, all the while with Jasper patting his mother's hand.

As soon as we entered my territory, we were surrounded by fifteen bikes. They paved the way to the hospital. My son sat in the back seat with my wife's head in his lap brushing her hair back, his little voice murmuring words of encouragement to her.

Yeah, I was teaching my boy right.

Fifteen hours later, the MC princess made her way into the world as quiet as her momma, and as hellacious as her too when her temper was riled.

Cassidee Kalani O'Malley weighed in at six pounds nine ounces. She had her momma's hair color and she had my eyes. For the third time in my life, I fell in love all over again. I felt like instead of having one heart, I had three, because the three of them owned my whole heart.

Had I ever imagined that my entire house would be filled to the brim with little Harleys and a lot of blue and pink? I wouldn't change it for the world.

Two Years Later

I looked up when I sensed that two pieces of my heart were walking toward me.

The club was having a party for Cassidee's two-year-old birthday. To say she had been spoiled by her aunts and uncles had been an understatement.

Cotton had a plate in one hand, and something rolled up under his arm. In his other arm was a tightly wrapped sleeping Cassidee. Daddy's little princess and

Mommy's little spitfire. She was the apple in Jasper's eye. Lord help the boy who tried to measure up to Jasper because they wanted to have Cassidee.

Jasper and Cassidee already had all the men bowing to do their bidding. And it didn't hurt that all of them would die for my babies and I would do the same for all of them. Family.

But I knew it then like I knew it now—it was going to take a special kind of woman to win over my son, Jasper. We were the apples of his eye. He was only six years old, but he could beat the best of them. When you had a father like Cotton, and uncles like York, Garret, Cooper, Xavier, and Knox, you learned a thing or two. Add to the fact their grandfather spoiled them ridiculously.

But something that was so ironic and proved that fate worked in mysterious ways. Cassidee's favorite animal . . . is a unicorn. She had even squealed when Cotton put a unicorn's horn on our rottweiler we named Nella.

For the people who say that breed is vicious, do they have family videos of a two-year-old clinging to the scruff of a dog who had a pink horn on its head as she was running around the backyard making that two-year-old squeal with delight? And did she ever allow her to fall? Nope, Nella twisted her body every which way so that Cassidee never fell.

I was talking to Marley, liking the fact that I now had another ole' lady to talk to too. I had been there the day the shit hit the fan in the clubhouse with York.

I still couldn't get over the past that York and Marley shared. I couldn't imagine that happening to Cotton and myself.

And Marley wasn't the only addition we added to our family.

When Cotton set the plate down in front of me, I smiled as wide as the blue yonder.

"Cheesecake," I murmured. Oh, the powers of cheesecake.

He leaned down, moved my raven black hair off my shoulder, and kissed me behind my ear, where I had placed an intricate K. It symbolized us—a K for Kane and a K for Kitten. His Kitten. On my right wrist I had the two letters J and C intertwined in a tribal script so that it looked like a bracelet with their initials on the top. It was my favorite tattoo.

With stars in his eyes, all because he was staring at me, as he would say, Cotton handed me the piece of parchment paper after he unrolled it for me.

The words 'National Star Registry' became unveiled.

And there, halfway down the page, was a star. 'Novalie's Star', the heading read, and below that, a subtext layer read, 'My Kitten, My Heart'.

And that night, beneath the stars in our hammock in the backyard after we had laid Jasper down to sleep beside Cassidee in their little tent, Cotton showed me where my star was, then we made love like it was the very first time.

"I love you, Kane," I whispered in his ear.

"Love you too, Kitten. I'm so ready for the next fifty years with you." Of that, he was true.

"Bullshit," I threw at him, he tossed his head back and roared with laughter.

And at the worst possible moment, our daughter had apparently woken up and exited the tent, then said her first word ever,

"Bullshit," but without the B and part of the 'shit', came from our precious little two-year-old Cassidee.

Twelve Years Later

"You watch your six, sweetheart. You think smart. You bring your ass home safely to me." Novalie was a nervous wreck. Her baby was shipping out for basic training after he joined the Army the day he turned eighteen.

Since we lived close to one of the stations for training, he hitched a ride with one of his friends who was also a kid with one of our chapters.

They had met in high school and they'd been best friends ever since.

"Y'all watch each other's sixes. I mean it. Your grandfather would have been so proud of you. While you're over there, he'll be watching down on you." Novalie's father had passed away two years ago. Sadly, the cancer came back after him at full force. He just didn't have enough strength when it hit him to fight it all.

"Mom, we'll be fine. Love you." I could tell that it was taking my boy all he had to not break down himself.

"Love you too, sweetheart." My wife was one second away from losing it.

"Love you, big bro." Our daughter, Cassidee, thought her daddy and her brother walked on water. And she, well, she still got away with everything no matter what she did.

"Love you too, munchkin." It was going to be weird not having Jasper in the house. But it was going to be something entirely different for Cassidee to not have her big bro there.

Most siblings were so different, even without an age gap. My kids? They did everything together. If Jasper went somewhere, he took his sister with him. If Cassidee wanted to watch a girly film, my boy would tell his friends what was up and he would be right there on the couch holding the popcorn so they both had easy access.

Was I okay that my children were spoiled? Absolutely.

And what I had also noticed was that my little girl, well, my fourteen-year-old daughter, also had a look in her eyes whenever she saw Jasper's best friend, Clip.

Still to this day, even after nineteen years, whenever Novalie dressed in sweatpants, a tank, and a messy bun, it was all I could do to keep my hands from roaming her body.

Novalie

That same look I gave Cotton when I first saw him, I still wore on my face nineteen years later when I looked at him.

"You come back safe. You write. You don't make your mother worry," Cotton said to our son.

"Yes, sir. Love you, Dad." They did a one-arm manly hug.

"Love you, son." For the fifth time in my life, I saw my husband getting teary-eyed. It didn't happen often, it only happened when something was important to him, his kids, or me.

When they climbed into the truck, we stayed there until we could see their tail lights no longer.

"Love you, Kane," I whispered in his ear.

"Love you too, Kitten," he whispered in my ear.

"Guys? Do y'all have to be that dang mushy. Y'all are married and old," our daughter said from behind us.

And my husband just couldn't help himself. He dipped low, tossed me over his shoulder, smacked my ass, all with Cassidee grumbling and my husband rolling with laughter all the way to the front door.

I would never trade what I had for a second because what I had was perfect.

Cotton always said I was his savior. But he had it dead wrong.

He is my savior.

Thank You

Oh, my freaking goodness!!! I can't believe this book is already over. Cotton and Novalie wanted their love story and I'm so happy that they chose me to write it for y'all. I sincerely hope that you enjoyed this book and you fell in love with them right along with me.

Xoxo,

Tiffany Casper

Other Works

Wrath MC
Mountain of Clearwater

Clearwater's Savior

Clearwater's Hope

Clearwater's Fire

Clearwater's Miracle

Clearwater's Treasure

Clearwater's Luck (TBD)

Clearwater's Redemption (TBD)

Christmas in Clearwater (TBD)

Dogwood's Treasures

Dove's Life

Phoenix's Plight

Raven's Climb (TBD)

DeLuca Empire

The Devil & The Siren

The Cleaner & The Princess (TBD)

Novellas

Hotter Than Sin (Free eBook with Newsletter)

Silver Treasure (Feb 2021)

The Rancher's Heart (TBD)

Connect With Me

My Website

https://tiffanycasper.com

Facebook

https://www.facebook.com/author.tiffany.casper

Instagram

https://www.instagram.com/authortiffanycasper/

Goodreads

https://www.goodreads.com/author/show/19027352.Tiffany_Casper

Made in the USA
Middletown, DE
18 February 2025